Tales From The Crows
A Collection of Horror Stories

CL LaVigne

Cover Designed by MiblArt

Tales From the Crows

A Collection of Horror Stories

www.cllavigne.com

www.facebook.com/CLLaVigneAuthor

ISBN (paperback): 979-8-9884845-1-6

ISBN (e-book): 979-8-9884845-2-3

Contents

Special thanks to my readers who helped select three of the stories that appear in this collection; and to Melodye and Andrea who provided the winning story ideas.
Your support is priceless!

Josephine the Crow

Crows represent physical or spiritual change. They also carry messages from the Divine.

Josephine the crow is my spirit animal. She has been with me a long time and even followed us when we moved. I've watched her raise her babies for four years. To me, the most beautiful sound is when she stands at the top of a tree and calls out to her sons and daughters or, on occasion, she sings to me.

During those intimate chats, she shared the stories you see within these pages.

Enjoy!

Sacrifice

Hoo-who. Hoo-who.

The owl's forlorn call drifted through the Forgotten Land, so named because its location was erased from all maps a century earlier. In the years that followed, references to the remote area were forbidden, and children were banned from venturing past Heron Marsh, a natural aquatic border separating the town of Brumble from the Forgotten Land.

It was too dangerous.

The forest had been cursed.

Although forgotten, the forbidden land pulsed with life. Supernatural life if you were to believe the townsfolk. Groves of oaks, pines and cedars sheltered thick bushes ripe with berries. Rare and unusual flowers that had found the perfect mix of shade and sun thrived in the rich loamy soil. Wildlife of every shape and size roamed the thick woodland. Villagers gossiped about seeing giant deer, six-feet tall at the shoulder, standing at the edge of the tree line gazing across the watery expanse of Heron Marsh.

Late at night chilling howls would arise from the Forgotten Land causing the people of Brumble to shutter their houses well before the first shadow of darkness crept across their thresholds. If a soul ventured outside after the night gripped the land, they did so in the company of others and usually around the protection of the community fire.

Legends and myths ran rampant, especially one account of an ancient mausoleum having been constructed in the middle of the cursed land. Supposedly, this building housed an evil entity, a demon so vile, the tomb had been sealed with magic to prevent its release.

But it was only a rumor.

Mother Dugan, Brumble's revered storyteller, delighted in spinning this tale around the campfire while the young and old huddled close to one another, fearful that the words conjured from the past would encourage spirits to materialize beside them.

On one such night, just after the harvest had been brought in from the fields, and after everyone had eaten their fill, Mother Dugan perched on a large tree stump and motioned for the people to sit.

"Let me tell you about the sad tale of the Sweeten sisters," she teased as she grinned her Jack-o'-lantern smile.

The flickering flames of the campfire cast shifting shadows across her face and contributed to the mood of horror and mystery. She studied the group assembled before her and narrowed her eyes at the young ones, which made them curl into the protective arms of their mothers and fathers. The older ones, those that had heard the tale for years, sat far away from the fire's light. Tiny toddlers, no more than four-years-old, huddled together at Mother Dugan's feet.

"Let me tell you about the Anniversary of the Sacrifice and how the Forgotten Land came to be," the storyteller began in a low, serious tone. "It all began with twin sisters and the sacrifice they made to keep Brumble safe from evil." She paused for dramatic effect and sipped her warm cider before continuing.

"Marcy and Angie Sweeten were orphaned at the age of fourteen when their mother died of the fever." Mother Dugan poked the fire with a long stick and watched the sparks scatter up into the night sky. "Their father had passed the year before in a tragic accident. With no other kin to care for them, the girls set their minds on fending for themselves. The house was in decent shape despite a few leaks in the roof. The chickens continued to lay eggs and the cow still gave milk. Their small kitchen garden provided enough food for them to survive. There was nothing else they needed.

"They were practical and determined young women."

She sipped her cider and peered at the children from over the rim of the mug. With wide eyes and attentive faces, she could see they were caught on the tale's hook and wanted more.

"The girls were resourceful. Using the herbal recipes that had been in their family for generations, they built a thriving business on potions and salves from the herbs and flowers that grew in the surrounding woodlands. Just like their parents, they were accomplished practitioners of the ancient healing ways and offered their services to the sick and injured by casting spells and dispensing carefully prepared elixirs."

A young blonde girl of four raised her hand. "Did they go to the Forgotten Land for herbs?"

Mother Dugan smiled gently at the sweet child's question. "Yes. When the Sweetens lived here, there was no curse upon the land, which was known then as Durrant Woods, named after the family that owned and shared the riches of the woodland. The Durrants invited the townsfolk to boat across the marsh and forage for whatever they needed."

A low murmur of wonderment rose from the assembled crowd.

Mother Dugan cleared her throat. "Five years passed. The sisters were now nineteen and had grown into beautiful women, the spitting image of their dearly departed mother—green eyes, auburn hair, and petite figures. They had grown into capable witches and used their magical powers for the benefit of the townsfolk who regarded the sisters as being of pure heart and mind.

Qualities that many yearned for.

"One day, a stranger approached Brumble. This traveler carried no knapsack nor did he possess any worldly goods, for he was merely a shadow person who had entered our world from the realm of the demons. His intent was to cause chaos in our peaceful village by stealing the magic of the Sweeten sisters."

The storyteller leaned forward and pointed her gnarled finger at the little girl in the front row. The child shrunk back against her brother who wrapped his arms around her in a bear hug.

"Since the Sweeten house had been built on the edge of town, the enchanted young man could easily knock upon their door while remaining unseen by others. When Marcy appeared in the entryway, he cast a diabolical spell causing her to fall madly in love with him. Despite the protection symbols etched into the door frame, the demon knew that if Marcy invited him inside, the protection magic would be instantly broken. Compelled by the young man's sorcery, she gestured for him to enter the home.

"That...was...a...mistake." Mother Dugan spat out each word as if they were poison.

"Angie was in a nearby village tending to a sick friend. When she arrived home later that night, she found the desiccated remains of Marcy slumped in a chair. All her magical essence had been sucked away. The evil entity stood nearby and glared at Angie with blood-red eyes."

Mother Dugan stopped, drank her cider, and smacked her lips.

"At an early age, Angie had demonstrated the gift of psychic sight, telling her parents about the spirits who hovered around her, talking to her and sharing secrets of life beyond the veil. To help her understand these encounters, her father, who was also a sensitive, instructed her on the various good and evil beings that inhabited both worlds.

"It was this six sense that immediately alerted Angie to the evil entity that had invaded her home and taken her sister's life. To Angie, he did not appear as a young man. He appeared in her mind's eye as a dark, hairy beast swaddled in the foul stench of death. He stepped toward her, but she bolted out the front door and ran toward Durrant Woods seeking protection within the sacred land.

"At that time, it was well known that Durrant Woods swirled with an incredible positive energy. No emissaries of evil could penetrate the boundaries of its protective power. Angie raced toward the woodland knowing her life depended on her reaching the sanctuary. When she reached the edge of the marsh, the skiff normally moored on the bank was missing.

"She glanced over her shoulder. The determined young man walked quickly toward her, his eyes glowing red. She had no choice. She kicked off her shoes, plunged into the marsh, and swam toward Durrant Woods. The stretch of water to the edge of the woodland was twenty-five feet away, and Angie swam as fast as she could until her feet touched the bottom just six feet from shore. When she stood up, the muck sucked her down until she was mired up to her thighs. The more she struggled, the more she sank into the muddy bottom until she couldn't move.

"She heard splashing. Turning around, she spied the entity walking on top of the water. A wicked grin filled his face. Angie gasped at the rows of razor-sharp teeth lining his jaws, and she struggled furiously to escape him, but the mud sucked her down even deeper. Just when Angie was sure the demon would grab her, a miracle occurred."

Mother Dugan paused to refill her mug from a jug that sat on the ground beside the stump. She eyed the astonished faces in the crowd. As though a huge wind had pushed them from behind, the people leaned forward to catch every detail of the story.

A young boy walked before her and quietly asked, "What was the miracle, Mother Dugan? Did Angie escape the demon?"

The boy's innocence squeezed her heart so much that her eyes watered with tears of joy. She patted his head and replied, "Yes and no."

The lad cocked his head like a puppy. "What do you mean, Mother Dugan?"

"The demon snatched Angie by her long, beautiful auburn hair and yanked. With her body stuck securely in the muck, Angie couldn't move. So, when the entity pulled her long tresses, her hair pulled away from her scalp. The bloody mess dangled from the entity's hand as he cackled at her."

"Ewww," the children squealed.

"Pain flooded Angie's brain. And along with the agony rose a fury she didn't know existed. Before she realized what was happening, she shoved her hands toward the grinning demon and spoke aloud a banishment spell created by her great-great grandmother. She summoned the spirits of the north, the east, the south, and the west. She called upon the gods and goddesses of the heavens and the earth to assist her in banishing the evil that stood before her.

"The entity laughed and shook her bloody hair at her, taunting her and mocking her. As Angie rapidly spoke the incantation, the sky swirled dark and menacing. Then lightning stabbed the marsh as earsplitting thunderclaps followed seconds later. Hail stones mixed with rain pelted the marsh. But Angie continued weaving her magic, undeterred by the maelstrom that swirled above her.

"Suddenly a bolt of lightning zigzagged toward the demon. Because he was a shadow creature from a different realm, he easily dissipated into a puff of smoke to avoid being struck. At that moment, before he could transform back into a human figure, Angie used her magic to draw him into her mojo bag that she kept tied around her waist. The pouch jerked in her hands as the demon tried in vain to escape.

"During the magical downpour, the marsh had flooded enough to lift Angie from her mucky prison. She could now swim to the shoreline of Durrant Woods."

"Angie was saved!" the little boy shouted as he jumped up and down with joy. Mother Dugan patted his head and nodded.

"But that's not the end of the tale," she cautioned. "Angie made it safely to the edge of the shoreline soaked and tired. The skies cleared as her conjured storm raced away into the heavens. But she had a conundrum. Do you remember that evil entities could not set foot upon Durrant Woods because of the pure positive energy that flowed throughout that area? While Angie could step onto the land, the pouch containing the entity could not. Plus, the magic of her mojo bag would contain the demon for only four hours.

"She had a dilemma. She couldn't take him into the woodland, and if she turned back to the village, she feared the evil entity would escape and terrorize the town.

"Mr. Durrant, the patriarch of the family that owned the woodland, had noticed the odd storm. He knew the turbulent weather was the result of magic and ventured out to find the conjurer. He wandered to the shoreline and found Angie standing waist deep in the water. Exhausted and crying she explained her situation. Mr. Durrant stroked his chin for several minutes before he snapped his fingers and announced he had a solution."

The storyteller snapped her fingers. Several of the smaller children jerked and squealed. Then they nervously giggled.

"A stone mausoleum stood in the center of the forest. Within the crypt lay the remains of several Durrant generations—all great and powerful witches and sorcerers who had committed their lives to fighting evil and sustaining peace. Their combined energy was so immense that a force field emanated from the structure ten feet around all sides. Mr. Durrant told Angie that if he could get the demon into the mausoleum, the supernatural spirits of his ancestors would ensure the demon could never escape."

"But the demon can't go on the land," the little boy corrected.

Mother Dugan smiled lovingly at the youngster. "Ah, you're paying attention. That is most excellent. You are right, the demon cannot go on land even if he is contained within the magical bag because the positive energy would repel him immediately. What do you think Mr. Durrant did?"

The young boy shrugged. He glanced back toward his sister who also shrugged. "I don't know. What did he do?"

Mother Dugan took a drink of her cider and then cleared her throat. "What is evil?" The little ones shook their heads. "It is the absence of goodness and light. It is the realm of wickedness and darkness. So, if the evil entity could be enshrouded in a vessel of pure goodness and light, it could be safely transported to the mausoleum and sealed inside.

"Mr. Durrant pointed at Angie and explained that she was that vessel. She was pure of heart and mind, and represented goodness. If she consumed the demon's essence, they would have enough time to reach the mausoleum. But Mr. Durrant was conflicted because if Angie agreed to ingest the demon, she would forever be sealed in the crypt. She would be the eternal receptacle for evil and could never leave the tomb."

"But Angie can't die," wailed the little boy who placed his head against Mother Dugan's leg. She tousled his brown curls and cooed at him.

"But evil can't be released upon her neighbors in Brumble, can it?" The little boy swiped the tears from his cheeks and slowly nodded. "No, of course not. Angie knew what needed to be done. She told Mr. Durrant that she would agree to be the vessel for the demon on one condition. Durrant Woods must be forgotten and eliminated from the maps. People could no longer visit or forage. The Durrant family would continue on as the stewards of the woodland but it would be off limits to all others.

"Mr. Durrant pondered her terms. He admired the fortitude of the nineteen-year-old standing before him. She had a full life before her and, yet, she was choosing to spend her remaining years locked in a mausoleum holding the evil essence within her body. After much consideration, he nodded.

"Angie agreed that it was the only solution available to her.

"She held the magic bag up to her mouth and widen the opening just enough to cover her lips. She closed her eyes and sucked as hard as she could. The wispy demon clawed at her throat as he was drawn inside her body. Gagging and coughing, Angie held her hand over her mouth to prevent the entity's escape. Mr. Durrant handed her a cup of clear water he had pulled from a nearby well, and she gulped it down hoping to eliminate any trace of the demon. She swiped her mouth with the back of her hand."

The storyteller paused. There wasn't a dry eye in the crowd. "But the story does have a happy ending," she said cheerfully.

"Mr. Durrant guided Angie to the mausoleum deep in the middle of the woods. It was an immense windowless structure built hundreds of years earlier of solid granite blocks. Moss and lichen grew in the crevices and various vines with multi-colored flowers snaked around the ancient building. Each stone block bore a unique symbol, an engraved marking that contributed its protective power to the crypt. The figure of a raven had been carved into the cornerstone above the formidable iron door that was fastened with three locks. Mr. Durrant removed the ring of keys from around his neck and carefully unlatched each lock with a loud *clunk.*

"The door squealed open and musty air from years past swirled outward. Angie gazed into the dark cell. Her psychic senses detected dozens of spiritual warriors lining the walls with their swords and muskets in their hands. They turned and looked at her with reverence, with an understanding of her selfless decision.

"One spirit curled his ghostly finger inviting her to enter. Angie hesitated, the shadows of doubt darkening her eyes. Once she stepped through the entranceway her fate would be forever sealed. She would never know the love of another person, nor would she ever hold and nurture a child.

"Silent and still, she hovered before the threshold.

"Mr. Durrant patted Angie's shoulder. He understood her trepidation. While it was ultimately her decision, he wanted to ensure she understood how her actions would impact the town. He explained that once she entered the crypt, she would be in the midst of royalty, selfless warriors like herself who fought bravely to ensure evil would never gain a foothold on this land. If she sacrificed her life, the supernatural soldiers would address her as the "regal sorceress, the green witch of Brumble" who had captured a demon and saved the town.

"Titles didn't impress Angie. Power and fame were the desires of others, but not for her. She yearned for a simpler life, an unfettered existence where she could come and go as she pleased. The young girl gazed into the tomb, shook her head, and faced Mr. Durrant."

The young boy in the front row jumped to his feet. "What did she do, Mother Dugan? She has to save our town!"

The old woman smiled kindly at the youngster's outburst and sipped her cider. "Yes, indeed. Angie needed to save Brumble. So, she offered Mr. Durrant a compromise."

"A compromise?" The child rolled the unfamiliar word along his tongue.

"Yes. She offered to spare the town of Brumble from carnage in exchange for one little thing."

"One little thing," the boy repeated under his breath as though he was repeating sacred words.

A wide grin sliced into Mother Dugan's face. The campfire shadows danced across her cheeks like the darkening clouds of an approaching thunderstorm. "What Mr. Durrant hadn't considered, and, most definitely, something Angie hadn't taken into account, was when she consumed the demon's essence, she also allowed the vile entity enough time to take over her body. Cell by cell, his soul merged with the young witch's lifeforce.

"Angie's eyes turned oily black as she sneered at Mr. Durrant. With a wave of her hand, the mausoleum's massive door slammed shut and locked as the ghostly ancestors howled warnings. Then she drew so near to the frightened farmer their noses almost touched as she whispered into his ear 'I will spare your town if you provide me one sweet soul every year on this day that will be known, henceforth, as the Anniversary of the Sacrifice.'"

"That doesn't make any sense," the little boy complained. "If Angie didn't take the demon into the crypt with her, Brumble wouldn't be saved." He nudged his fists on his hips and pouted.

"But Angie did save the town of Brumble," the storyteller soothed.

"How?" The child crossed his arms and stamped his foot demanding an answer.

A fearful murmur arose from the crowd as some parents scooped up their children and retreated to the wall that encircled the campfire. Mother Dugan followed their actions with narrowed eyes. "Silence!" she bellowed. "Be still and sit down. The story is not complete."

Her tongue, black and grotesque, lolled out of her mouth and slowly licked her cracked lips. Drool ran down her chin as she stared down at the toddlers huddled at her feet. Their pitiful wails prompted parents to hurry toward them, but Mother Dugan held up her hand. "Sit down," she ordered. Fearful mothers and fathers reluctantly returned to their seats, darting worried glances between their children and Mother Dugan.

"Now, for the rest of the story." The storyteller gazed into the blue eyes of the little boy and continued. "So, you see, my little one, a deal was struck and Angie was allowed to leave Durrant Woods to live her life.

"Evil never ventured into Brumble. The crops flourished, the people prospered, and life was glorious. Except for one little thing: the Anniversary of the Sacrifice, when Angie would stroll into town demanding her payment for keeping wickedness at bay.

"That day is today, my precious boy," The storyteller picked up the innocent child and placed him gently on her lap.

Muffled soft cries drifted through the assemblage, and the child turned toward the sound, "Momma?"

"There, there, little one. All will be okay," Mother Dugan said as she stroked the youngster's fine blonde hair. She began singing an ancient melody, magical words handed down from her ancestors. Hypnotized by the lyrical tune, the toddler soon grew sleepy, his eyelids opening and closing until they shut for the final time. His head drooped upon Mother Dugan's chest, and she smiled gently at the dozing child lying in her arms. "My brave little warrior, my innocent sacrifice," she cooed.

Mother Dugan mused about the time, one hundred years earlier, when she was known as Angie Sweeten and enjoyed an idyllic life with her twin sister, Marcy until evil had called upon them. Now, by a cruel twist of fate, her soul was forever intertwined with that wicked entity. On three-hundred and sixty-four days of the year, she was a peaceful, lovable storyteller. But on the Anniversary of the Sacrifice, evil came forth to collect its payment.

With coal-black eyes, Mother Dugan scanned the eerily quiet crowd. Suddenly she threw her head back, her chin jutting toward the sky as her head shook violently. Bones cracked and ligaments snapped as her mouth stretched tall and ripped sideways until she appeared only as a mouth with a body. Her lips curled upward and away from her needle-sharp teeth, and then, in one quick movement, she stuffed the precious little boy into her gaping maw.

Dead Air

This story was crafted from an idea submitted during a contest I held for my readers who voted on the submissions.

Congratulations, Melodye, for a great idea.

"9-1-1. What's your emergency?"

SNAP. CRACK.

The dispatcher glanced at her supervisor and repeated, "9-1-1. State your emergency."

A female voice faltered in the hissing static. Holding the headphones snug against her ears, the dispatcher strained to hear the words which floated in and out like a cry on the wind. "Hello? Is someone there?"

"Murder," croaked the raspy voice.

Dead air.

A shiver raced up the dispatcher's spine. "That voice is creepy. She says the same thing every time."

The supervisor studied the phone number. "Third call from that number this week."

"Should I notify the police?"

"We have to. It could be an actual emergency this time. Although my gut tells me it will be a false alarm like the other two times. Is it the same address?"

"Yes. Same address."

"Send the police."

"Yes, ma'am."

At three in the morning, the temperature hovered near eighty degrees in the Big Oaks neighborhood. The darkness swaddled the mansions in a muggy embrace. Nothing ever happened in this quiet gated community. No break-ins nor domestic violence. Not even childish pranks that had gone awry. It was an idyllic community to raise a family. The police had never been called in the five years since the developer drained the swamp, dumped truckloads of dirt, and constructed stylish homes.

Not until this week.

Officers Casey and Tandy sat in their patrol car outside 226 Raven Avenue and reviewed the details of the emergency call.

"Three times' the charm," Terry Tandy quipped. "Maybe we'll find a dead body this time."

"That's morbid," Jim Casey responded as he eyed the neighboring houses, scanned the yards, and searched the streets. His quick observation took a matter of seconds, but he absorbed all the pertinent details his trained mind could find.

It was quiet. A thick stillness filled the neighborhood with an eerie calm.

The officers sat in their car and peered at the two-story Colonial-style home from where the emergency call had been made. A flickering street light cast a hazy yellow glow across the front. Nicely manicured lawn and shrubs framed the white house that was accented with black shutters and trim. Two massive columns stood on either side of the entryway. The home sat silent and dark.

"It's quiet just like the other two times," Officer Casey observed. "How much you wanna bet we wake up Beverly Saunders, and she yells at us just like the previous visits?"

"She threatened to call our sergeant if we showed up again," Officer Tandy reminded his partner.

"Let's go. It's probably nothing, but we've gotta check." Jim Casey exited the car and patted his revolver three times, a tradition he picked up from his old man who was a retired policeman. The reasoning was never clear but his dad was adamant that touching your gun would guarantee you luck. There must be some truth to the superstition because his old man retired after thirty years of service and had never been shot.

Jim's gaze swept the grounds as they approached the house. A sudden movement snatched his attention. "Did you see that, Terry?"

"See what?"

"A light came on at the house next door. It flashed for a second, but now..."

"Officers." The urgent female voice spoke in low tones.

The men turned toward the sound. A figure walked briskly toward them, a hand waving in the air. "Officers," the female whispered as she drew near. "There's something very odd going on in that house." She jabbed her finger at the two-story Colonial.

"And, you are?" Officer Casey asked.

"Mason. Mrs. Mason. I live next door." Despite the warm temperature, she pulled her terry robe tighter around her thin body.

"I'm Officer Casey and this is my partner, Officer Tandy."

"Yes, I've seen you out here the other two times. You barely spent any time inside that house. I'm telling you, something is very strange there."

Officer Tandy opened his pocket and withdrew his notepad and pen. He raised an eyebrow at his partner. "What tells you something is odd about this house?" he asked.

"The yelling and the flashing lights."

"I don't hear anything. I don't see any lights," Officer Casey countered.

"Of course, you don't. Not now, silly. But when you're not here, I hear them arguing inside the house."

"Them?" Officer Tandy said as he scribbled a note.

"Yes. Them. I hear two voices talking to each other near the back of the house. Ever since that sister showed up. And the pool lights flash off and on like someone's playing with the light switch. It's like a damned disco." Mrs. Mason crept closer as if to share a secret. "My husband and I are seniors, you know. We need our sleep. Look at my eyes. And, my heart—"

Officer Tandy held up his pen. "Sister? I thought only Beverly Saunders lived here."

"Well, she does. But her sister came to visit last weekend. Beverly was having a pool built and I assumed her sister visited for a pool party or whatever. Her blue Chevy was parked on the street for days, and we don't do that sort of thing around here. We're a respectable community. We park our vehicles in the garage where they belong. Anyway, her car disappeared after the weekend, so I assumed she'd left. But now I hear two ladies arguing in the wee hours of the morning."

"What does the sister look like?"

"Well, let me see. I only saw her up close once when I stopped her outside and introduced myself. She looks almost identical to Beverly except Beverly has black hair and her sister has blonde hair. Badly bleached hair, I might add. But their height and weight are the same."

"Thank you for those details, Mrs. Mason. They were very helpful." Officer Tandy scribbled more notes.

"It's my duty as a good neighbor," Mrs. Mason proclaimed as she pushed her lower lip out and eyed both officers. "I may be retired but I can still do my part in ensuring our neighborhood stays safe."

"Yes ma'am," Officer Tandy responded as he closed his notepad and pushed it back into his pocket.

"Well, I'll leave you to your work, then." Mrs. Mason clutched her robe and ambled away, stopping occasionally to glance over her shoulder at the officers who remained on the sidewalk watching her go home. When she went inside Terry turned to Jim.

"That was interesting," he said. "I wasn't aware of a sister. Beverly never mentioned one when we asked if anybody else lived in the house."

"Well, let's go talk to her now and see what's up," Jim replied. The officers marched up the red-brick walkway that led to the front door like a red landing strip.

Jim touched his revolver as he pushed the doorbell.

No answer.

He pounded on the door with his fist. "Police!"

A light illuminated in an upstairs bedroom next door. The shadow of a head loomed in front of the window.

"Mrs. Mason is making sure we do our job," Officer Tandy said, a tone of sarcasm coloring his words.

Officer Casey prepared to pound the door again when the porch light came on and the door opened a few inches. A security chain stretched across the gap and a woman peered at them through the metal links. "Yes?"

"Ma'am," Officer Casey began. "We had an emergency call placed from this location. Please open the door."

"Again?" The woman sighed and slammed the door. A metallic rattling punctuated by several angry *shits* emerged from inside the house. Smirks spread across the officers' faces. They shifted their feet and stared at the ground.

After a few moments, the door opened wide. "Please come in," she said as she gestured toward the foyer.

"Good morning, Ms. Saunders," Officer Tandy said as he passed in front of her. He had retrieved his notepad and pen and waited by the wall in the foyer.

She mumbled something unintelligible and shuffled down the hallway leading into the kitchen. The officers didn't follow right away. She glanced back. "Come on, then. I need coffee this early in the morning." She gestured for them to follow her.

"Ma'am, is there anybody else in the house?" Officer Casey asked as he peered up the stairs that led upward from the kitchen.

"No," she replied curtly. "Just me. And I didn't make that call. Something must be wrong with my phone." She jerked her thumb at her mobile lying on the counter.

"Do you mind if I look at your phone?" Officer Tandy asked as he joined her in the kitchen. He glanced at his partner who marched up the stairs to the second floor.

"Go ahead. You won't find anything. You didn't last time either."

Officer Tandy scrolled through the phone log. There was no indication a call had ever been made to 9-1-1 from the phone. He bit his lower lip while wrestling with the possibilities.

"Do you want coffee?" she asked as she poured a cup for herself.

"No, ma'am. I'm good," he replied. He glanced into the darkened family room. "I'll just check the downstairs while my partner checks upstairs."

"Whatever," she responded, glaring at him over the rim of her mug.

The officers checked the entire house. All windows and doors were locked and there was no evidence anybody else lived there. They reconvened in the kitchen. Ms. Saunders sat on a bar stool, holding her coffee under her nose inhaling the steam. The two officers glanced at each other.

"Ma'am," Officer Tandy began. "This is the third time a call from this phone has come into our emergency department."

"Correction," she interjected. "The calls did not come from my phone. You've already checked." She slurped her coffee. "Have you ever considered someone is call spoofing the police department and trying to get me in trouble?"

"What about your sister?" Officer Tandy asked as he checked his notes.

Beverly's lips lingered on the rim of the cup as if they had been glued there. She glared at the officer through narrowed eyes, and then she slowly and deliberately placed her cup on the counter, folded her hands, and quietly asked, "My sister?"

"Yes, ma'am. Where is your sister?" The officers exchanged glances.

"She visited you last weekend. Is she still here?" Officer Casey chimed in.

Beverly stared at the counter, her mouth twitched and puckered as she considered the question. "Oh, you mean Angela!" Her response was loud, and Officer Casey's eyebrows arched at the surprising shift in tone. "Yes. She was here last weekend. But she's gone. She went home."

"Oh? What day did she leave?" Officer Tandy asked as he jotted a note.

Beverly poured a second cup of coffee and walked to the sliding doors leading to the pool deck. She turned on the floodlights which illuminated the pool in electric blue. She sipped and stared outside. "She left after the pool was complete. Tuesday maybe. We had a little celebration and then she went away."

Officer Tandy flipped through his notes. "We received the first call on Wednesday."

Officer Casey joined Beverly at the sliders and surveyed the screened area. Underwater shadows danced on the pool walls while the skimmer churned ripples on the surface. An explosion of blue bathed the pool deck with an otherworldly appearance. "Nice pool."

Beverly gazed outside. Her eyes stared downward toward the blue water. The rim of the coffee cup rested on her bottom lip.

"Ms. Saunders?"

"What? Oh, I'm sorry. I'm very tired. What did you say?"

"The pool. It looks incredible."

She nodded. "Yes. It was worth all the trouble." She sipped her coffee and suddenly perked up. "Are we done here? I need my sleep."

Officer Tandy closed his notepad and nodded at his partner. "Yes ma'am. We're done. Sorry to have troubled you."

The officers let themselves out as Ms. Saunders remained by the sliders. The front door clicked shut. She glanced over her shoulder to make sure they were gone, then a wide grin spread across her face.

She fixed her gaze on the luminescent blue water and placed her palm on the glass. "Shut up, Beverly," she growled. "Stop calling."

"I agree with Mrs. Mason," Terry uttered. "There's something really odd about that woman. But I can't put my finger on it."

"We searched everywhere. Nothing's out of place. Come on, partner. Let's go." He yanked the driver's side door opened and stopped. A sudden movement at the neighbor's house snatched his attention. He instinctively patted his gun three times.

"Terry, we have company." He poked his chin toward the yard next door.

Terry followed his partner's gaze. Mrs. Mason scurried down the sidewalk, her hands fluttering out to the side like a bird preparing to take flight. "Don't go. Don't go," she huffed as she shuffled to the cruiser.

"What's wrong?" Officer Tandy asked.

"She's talking to someone again. Right now, by the pool."

Officer Casey sighed audibly. "Mrs. Mason. People have a right to talk to themselves."

"No, she's not talking to herself. She's talking to another person. There are *two* voices. Come on, I'll show you."

Terry looked at his partner and shrugged before reluctantly following Mrs. Mason. Jim shook his head, slammed the car door, and chased after them. "Hold up, I'm coming."

Mrs. Mason led the officers into her house, up the stairs, and into the corner bedroom. From this vantage point, they could see clearly into Ms. Saunders' backyard. Mrs. Mason pointed toward Beverly's pool and handed Officer Casey the binoculars she kept on a nearby table. "Look down there. Look at her."

"Use these much?" He said bitingly as he lifted the binoculars to his face.

Mrs. Mason ignored his sarcasm and tapped her finger on the glass. "There...there."

Jim focused the binoculars, and his partner lifted the window so they could hear any conversation. Ms. Saunders circled the pool deck ranting and raving. A soft voice responded to her tirade while the floodlights flickered in spastic blue pulses. "Damn, it is like a disco party," he commented under his breath. "I hear a second voice but can't see another person."

"I never see another woman," Mrs. Mason confirmed. "But I always hear two distinct voices. Sometimes they're quite loud."

Beverly marched around the pool. She alternated between throwing her hands in the air and then pointing accusingly toward the water. "You're pissing me off," she seethed. She ran her fingers through her hair angrily, viciously raking her head from back to front. As her hands came forward, a black hairy mass pulled off her head and dangled from her fingers.

"Shit. She's pulling her hair out," Officer Tandy remarked.

"That's not her hair, partner." Officer Casey sharpened the focus on the binoculars. "That's a wig." He whirled toward Mrs. Mason. "The sister's hair is blonde, right?"

"A bad bleach-blonde," she replied. "She's got hideous dark roots."

Officer Casey turned to his partner. "Terry. That girl down there has blonde hair. She just took off a black wig."

"What are you saying?" Mrs. Mason exclaimed as she muscled her way to the window. She peered into the backyard, readjusted her glasses, and strained to see the woman by the pool. "Well, that's not Beverly. That's her sister, Angela."

"C'mon, partner. We need to pay Ms. Saunders another visit." Officer Casey handed the binoculars to Mrs. Mason.

The officers dashed next door. As Jim raised his fist to knock, a loud *clunk* caught them by surprise. Thinking Ms. Saunders had unlocked the door, they stepped back and watched expectedly. The door slowly swung open, revealing a wispy gray mist that hovered in the entryway for several seconds before hurrying down the hallway toward the sliding glass doors.

Jim patted his revolver and nodded at his partner. "Let's go, Terry."

Erratic blue flashes splashed the darkened interior as they hurried toward the pool. A woman stumbled around the deck, yelling obscenities and shaking the tattered black wig at the water.

"Get out of my life, you hag!" she screamed as she threw the hairpiece into the pool.

"Jim, look at that," Terry said as he tapped the glass with his finger. A wispy gray hand rose out of the water. The fingers elongated and teased the curls on the black wig before snatching it and yanking it underwater.

Their radios suddenly crackled to life. "Emergency call just received at 226 Raven Avenue claiming a murder. Second time tonight."

"10-4, we're on site," Terry replied.

"Copy." The dispatcher hung up.

Officer Casey glanced at Ms. Saunders' mobile phone lying on the kitchen counter. "No calls came from that phone. I wonder who called that in."

"Someone must be call spoofing the emergency department like Beverly suggested. But who?" Terry wondered aloud. The men stared at the bizarre scene on the other side of the sliders.

"Leave me alone, Beverly. What's done is done." Ms. Saunders knelt by the edge of the pool and slapped the surface with her hands. "Get over it, bitch, and leave me be!"

"Is that steam?" Jim pointed toward the other side of the pool where a wispy mass formed just above the water's surface.

The thick mist emerged from the deep end of the pool. A large white cloud at first, it soon twisted into an elongated shape as it drifted toward Ms. Saunders. As it drew near, it rose higher into the air until it hovered six feet above the woman who continued cursing and smacking the water, unaware of its presence.

As the stunned officers looked on, the misty shape morphed into an ethereal female form. The figure turned and looked at the officers. In the center of the spirit's face, where the mist was darker, an exaggerated grin parted the smoke.

"Aha, there you are!" Ms. Saunders exclaimed as she stood up and shook her finger at the wispy figure looming above her.

The mist enlarged to three times its original size and swirled like a miniature maelstrom before it pounced upon the woman and grabbed her with smoky tentacles. The ghostly arms multiplied and quickly wrapped around the woman's body and throat, gagging her garbled plea for help. Ms. Saunders struggled to fight off the hazy apparition, but its strength and mass overpowered her. It lifted her up and slammed her down into the middle of the water, dragging her all the way to the bottom.

A flurry of bubbles boiled at the surface.

The officers wrestled with the lock on the sliders, but it wouldn't budge. "Jim, look at that." Terry's voice quavered as he tapped his partner on the shoulder. "Look up. Quickly."

Jim's gaze was met by the haunting dark eyes of the misty figure that stood on the other side of the glass. She raised one finger and waggled it at the officers, seemingly scolding them for trying to open the door. Then the apparition whisked away and dove under the surface of the water again.

"Stand back, Terry. I'm going to get this door open," Jim cautioned as he withdrew his revolver. After three rounds, the glass shattered into hundreds of pieces.

The officers bolted to the pool. The misty apparition had vanished, but Ms. Saunders remained on the bottom and stared at them with wide, frightened eyes. Black curly hair floated from her open mouth.

"That damned wig has been stuffed down her throat!" Terry yelled as he jumped in and swam toward the woman who lay eight feet below the surface.

He grabbed her arms and yanked, but her body wouldn't move. Then he planted his feet and pulled both of her legs, but the woman remained stuck to the bottom. With his lungs bursting, he reluctantly swam back to the surface.

"It's like she's anchored to the bottom," he gasped. "I'll try again." He gulped a deep breath and dove back in. When he reached her, a white film had formed over her eyes. This time as he pulled at her, she easily floated into his arms and he pushed her to the surface.

"An ambulance is on its way," Jim said as he grabbed Ms. Saunders and rolled her onto her back. Vacant eyes in a chalk-white face returned his stare. The matted black wig protruded from her mouth like a monstrous creature. He grabbed the curly hairs, yanked, and held it up. Long strands of mucous dripped to the pool deck. He grimaced and tossed it away.

"Beginning compressions," he called out as he began CPR.

Terry watched his partner press on Ms. Saunders chest in a steady rhythm. "Jim, she's gone. She's already blue and look at her bruised neck. It looks like she's been strangled."

"I've...got...to...try," Jim huffed.

Their radios crackled again. "Be advised another call has just been received from your location. The message is odd. The caller said 'look under the pool'"

Jim stopped pumping and stared at his partner.

Two days later, after the pool at 226 Raven was drained and the concrete was broken apart, Mrs. Mason watched the activity from the perch of her bedroom window. Yellow crime scene tape fluttered in the breeze as construction workers methodically removed chunks of concrete and steel rods. Piece by piece, all remnants of the once magnificent pool were loaded onto front end loaders that carried the debris to waiting dump trucks.

"Hold up!" Detective Andrews yelled to the army of workers. He had assumed command of the investigation after the drowning death of Angela Saunders. He hitched up his dress pants and hunkered down. After studying the ground in front of him, he swiped at the dirt with his gloved hand.

The mood was grim. Nobody dared to speak.

After a long minute he stood up and motioned for the forensics team to approach. "Found a body. Bring your gear."

Mrs. Mason sharpened the image on her binoculars. "Get out of the way. I can't see what's going on." She stomped her foot in frustration.

The workers solemnly filed out of the backyard leaving members of the police department to manage the scene. Officers Casey and Tandy stood nearby and observed the team members maneuver around the open hole.

"I still can't get the images out of my head," Terry whispered. "Ghosts aren't real...are they?"

"If you had asked me a week ago if I believed in spirits, I'd say you were nuts. But after what we saw and experienced, I don't know, Terry. I know what I saw and I hope I never experience it again."

"They found something." Terry pointed toward Detective Andrew who extracted an object from the hole and carefully placed it into an evidence bag held by Officer Thomas.

"Get that to the lab, stat!" the detective barked.

Jim hailed Officer Thomas as he approached them. "Hold up, Robert. What did they find?"

The officer held the plastic bag up in front of their faces. "It's a cellphone. It's in pretty good condition despite being mashed into the mud." He turned the bag so the screen was visible. "And it's still got a charge. Look, the screen lights up and look what appears...9-1-1."

"I'll be damned," Jim said to Terry. "Was Beverly making those calls?" The men gazed toward the pit where crime scene workers scurried around like ants.

On the edge of the mound just behind Detective Andrews stood a wispy gray figure. Initially a mass of billowing smoke, it twisted and contorted until a solid gray form of a woman with black hair materialized. She stared at Officers Casey and Tandy and smiled gently. She nodded at them and then evaporated before their eyes. Wispy specks separated and twirled upward into the sky.

"What'cha lookin at?" Robert asked as he followed their gaze.

Jim and Terry didn't respond.

They turned and walked away while Jim patted his revolver three times.

The Magic Thief

A voiding the spotlight of the full moon, Billy "The Tooth" Taylor lurked in the shadowed fringes of the graveyard. A thief and a murderer, Billy trusted the comfort of the darkness, a shadowy companion to many of the unholy creatures that slithered in search of blood or mayhem.

Midwinter held the land in its icy grip. A sudden gust of chilled air yanked the remaining leaves from the branches and tossed their desiccated remains against the tombstones. Their rustling screams echoed throughout the cemetery.

Billy shivered and tightened his tattered jacket around him with gnarled fingers that twisted at odd angles, a result from having been snapped too many times. A sane man wouldn't be standing in a cemetery in the middle of a freezing night. A sane man would be home eating hot strew, drinking a tankard of ale, and warming his hands by a fire.

But Billy wasn't sane. Hell, Billy wasn't even alive.

The memory of his death was like peering through cobwebs as bits of scenes clung together precariously, slowly unraveling and dissipating with each passing day. The fatal blow—a rough-edged brick slammed into the center of his face, right between the eyes—may have been delivered by a jealous rival, but something more cruel and heinous occurred after his attacker skittered away into the night.

A lone dark figure emerged from the shadows and approached Billy's battered body. Hovering his hands over the broken remains, the stranger summoned his dark magic to find a life force. But only the frigid essence of death responded.

He bent down to Billy's ear and whispered, "What is the price of life worth to you?"

Silence.

"I know you're in there, Billy. I ask you again, what is the price of life worth to you?" The dark man slammed his hands together and then thrust them toward the sky.

Stirred by the stranger's conjuring, the wind gusted through the trees and strummed the thin branches like strings on a rough-hewn guitar. Squeals and squeaks filled the air, and somewhere in the melody, the stranger received the answer he anticipated. He smiled to himself before hefting the carcass of broken bones over his shoulder and striding off into the darkness.

Billy was dead, but would soon be something worse.

The miserable memory stabbed Billy in the gut and he shivered again.

Billy didn't remember saying anything, but his master would later explain his answer was carried on the wind during the moment his last breath escaped and joined his soul in the ether.

And, his price for life? The dark man regenerated him. He stitched muscles together, fused jagged edges of bones, and filled his pummeled body with a new life force—an unholy blood which compelled Billy to carry out his master's immoral commands.

Billy danced somewhere between the realm of the grave and the illumination of life. Like a living person, he could feel the cold, be hungry, and even have emotions. As a non-living servant to his master, he constantly lived in the torment and despair of one who would never rest in the cold earth, nor ascend to an ethereal plane to join those who had passed before him.

It was the price he had paid for coming back from the dead. The master owned him and there was now an important job for him to complete.

Billy glanced up at the moon high above him. His eyes, blind and opaque like webbed marbles, swiveled about in their sockets searching for signs of the Guardian Crows: the loyal and fierce protectors of the graveyard.

Like a drunkard, his head jerked from side to side, and Billy knew, from the sudden lurching motion, that his master had claimed control of his body like a gamer with a joystick. Billy hated when the master took over his body, not that there was really much left of it to control. Two white orbs floated in a melted mass of red flesh. The gash that had been his mouth twisted down in a permanent sneer. Fleshy points on either side of his head appeared more like flaps than ears.

Using powerful mind magic, the dark man could now peer through Billy's sightless eyes. The master summoned his powers to detect the elemental spirits that could easily cloak their whereabouts. The Guardian Crows were soldiers for the elementals and were so black, only the glint of the moon's light on their black eyes could betray their location.

Move toward the hallowed ground, the master commanded.

The words drifted through Billy's brain as if they were his own thoughts. He had no choice but to obey. Under the control of the dark man, he lumbered into the clearing and turned toward the Seyler family plot. As Billy stretched his hands forward, the dark man conjured small beams of green light that streamed from Billy's fingertips. The magical lasers scanned the area for the Guardians Crows and elementals who had sworn oaths to protect this sacred space.

The Seyler family plot was a modest patch of ground in a larger cemetery. Four white marble obelisks marked the corners of the compass: north, east, south, and west. Within this space, and surrounding the family headstones, were stone pillars holding large urns etched with the Greek symbols for earth, air, fire, and water. The Seyler magical energy pulsed around the gravestones and, like a strong heartbeat, it ebbed and flowed with positive energy spreading out to the surrounding area like gentle waves.

SNORT!

Billy froze. The sudden noise emanated from the north entrance to the family plot. He swiveled his head so his master could listen carefully. Moments passed and the night grew silent once again.

Onward, the dark man directed. Billy grunted and staggered toward the north gate, his hands outstretched, his fingers probing and searching. *Stop!* The yell resonated in his head.

The master knew they had reached the protection zone of the sacred space. Invisible to the naked eye, the energy field surrounding the family plot flowed through, below and above the hallowed ground. Fiercely protected by the Guardian Crows and the elementals, the graveyard was impenetrable. Unless you happen to know magic.

The dark man *was* magic.

He commandeered Billy's mouth, twisting the lips rapidly as he directed Billy to speak an ancient incantation in a breathy whisper. Then he beckoned Billy to raise his arms to cast a spell. His hands swept clockwise, down and around, drawing a series of circles connected by magical sigils that glowed a greenish hue from the master's power.

Snow drifted down from the dark sky, a sign that the master's spell was materializing. A fine white powder coated the cemetery and everything around it. It drifted onto the trees and covered the Guardian Crows in a sleepy blanket. They ruffled their feathers and drifted off into a forced slumber that impacted every living creature in the cemetery.

Except for Billy, of course.

Now it was time for him to get to work and finish the job.

Listen carefully, Billy, the dark sorcerer urged. *Follow these instructions. You must go to each obelisk, find the secretive latch and open the hidden vault. Once done, you will extract the ceremonial tool and carefully place it into your bag.* Billy nodded and patted the leather satchel strapped around his body.

"Yes, master," he croaked in a hoarse whisper. Guided by the dark man, Billy grabbed the cold wrought iron gate leading into the family plot. His hands vibrated on the cold steel as the protective energy bit and stung his fingers like angry wasps.

He instinctively snatched his hands away.

Don't be afraid, his master reassured. *The Seyler magic won't hurt you because you're human. Move through the gate. Be quick about it now. We don't have much time.*

Billy gathered his courage and reached toward the ironwork. Working quickly, he unfastened the latch and swung the gate open, which groaned in protest. As he ambled into the sacred space, a warm energy washed over him, and he felt welcomed and loved. Billy sighed. The energetic caresses released his emotions and forgotten memories. He felt as though he was finally home and yearned to sit among the headstones.

The master jerked Billy out of his reverie. *Billy! Be sharp. You have to break the energy grid now. Remember your instructions. Go to the first obelisk quickly.*

Billy reluctantly lumbered to the six-foot, white marble structure located in the north corner. It marked the boundary of Jenny Seyler's tomb. Although he was blind, he sensed he was near someone important. Images flooded his brain. The memories carried forgotten details from his past: being whipped on a public street as a young boy, the kindness of a woman in a green dress, and the name Jenny Seyler.

Billy! the master angrily screamed in his mind. *Get on with it!*

Billy jolted into action as if poked with a cattle prod. Hands stretched out, he moved his arms back and forth until he finally bumped into the monument. Something caught the master's eye. *Billy, look toward the ground. What's that at the base of the obelisk?*

Billy cocked his head toward the ground as the Master commanded. There, under a dusting of snow, peacefully slept a small figure. *A guardian gnome*, growled the Master. *Vile, weak creatures. And, it's a lowly garden gnome. I can't believe he was assigned to guard such an important tomb.*

Billy didn't choose sides when it came to the bitter relationship between his master and the elementals. Billy was only a human, albeit dead. The gnome snoring by Billy's feet looked harmless. It appeared like a cute garden statue he had seen in people's yards when he was a boy. A tall red hat poked upward from its head and he wore a forest-green vest over brown woolen pants.

SNORT!

The gnome squirmed against the obelisk and eventually went back to sleep.

Forget the stupid gnome, Billy. Find the secret compartment, the dark man commanded.

At the top of the structure was a large marble sphere perfectly balanced on the sharp point of the triangular base. Circles were lightly etched into the sphere. Billy raised his right hand and the pulsating stream of green light scanned the obelisk.

I'll watch for the symbols to light up and, when I see a green flash, I'll let you know you've found the button to unlock the hidden compartment, the master advised.

Billy began at the top and slowly lowered his hand down one side as the magic beam showered the marble with an eerie greenish glare. Symbols illuminated briefly but there was no flash. He scanned the other two sides. When he reached the bottom of the third side, a small green flash appeared halfway down.

Push on it, the master commanded as he maneuvered Billy's hand to the location where the green flash occurred. When his finger depressed the symbol, there was a slight resistance before a triangular door slid open and revealed the contents inside: a small crystal orb.

An undine princess gave this orb to Jenny for saving her from a brutal fisherman, the dark master explained. *Don't drop it. This crystal gave Jenny the ability to gaze into the future.*

Billy carefully placed the three-inch ball into the leather pouch slung across his chest. An immediate shift in energy washed over him, and he wobbled as though he walked upon the deck of a storm-tossed ship. Billy knew he was a party to something evil but was powerless to do anything about the situation.

No time to waste, the master urged. *The sleeping spell won't last long. You need to retrieve the other tools from the other three obelisks.*

Billy glanced down at the slumbering gnome who clasped his hands across his chest and breathed deeply. A pang of jealousy bubbled up. Billy hadn't slept in years.

Billy! the dark man barked. *Move now!* Billy's head ached horribly from his master's constant screams. The headache made him nauseous, and he lightly touched his roiling stomach. Despite his pain, he lumbered onward toward the second obelisk. After a few steps, his feet entangled with something hard, and he face-planted into the frozen earth.

You fool, you tripped over Grace's grave!

Baby Grace lived only four days on this earthly plane. She was the first one to be buried in the Seyler family plot, and a small cherub statue marked her grave. A simple inscription on her headstone read:

> *Baby Grace Seyler*
> *Born Apr. 4 1870*
> *Died Apr. 8 1870*

While the master screamed a litany of curses in his head, Billy rubbed his throbbing ankle that had collided with the cherub statue.

You stupid lump! We're running out of time. Get your ass moving or the Guardian Crows will peck your eyes out!

A dead person possesses only one speed, and that is slow.

Spurred on by the dark man's threats, Billy stood up clumsily and teetered to the next pillar while waving his arms in front of him. He located the monument when his right hand smacked against its hard surface. The blow caused one mangled finger to break off and fall to the ground.

Idiot! the voice in his head yelled.

Billy hugged the structure to maintain his balance. As with the first obelisk, Billy stretched his hand forward so the master could scan the marble sides for the symbols that would unlock the secret door. This time when Billy opened the hidden compartment, he found a long, wooden stick. As the dark man gazed at it through Billy's eyes, he recognized it as a twelve-inch wand made of alder wood with a nugget of amethyst fastened into one end.

This was Jenny's tool for visiting the different dimensions, the master described.

Billy swiftly placed the item into his bag.

The energy shifted again, but this time it felt as though the earth tilted on its axis. Billy lurched sideways and struggled to maintain his balance as he wobbled toward the third pillar located in the southern part of the family plot. Familiar with the process now, Billy easily scanned the third obelisk, which soon yielded its prize: a brass candle with a blue flame. Billy was startled to find a burning candle sealed in a marble tomb.

*Be careful of this tool, it is the perpetual flame of truth. Don't gaze into its brilliance lest you fall under its spell, t*he master cautioned.

Billy averted his eyes and carefully lifted the candle out of the monument. The light shone brighter and higher as it emerged from its protective receptacle. The blue glow was mesmerizing and, although he couldn't see it, Billy felt compelled to turn his head and gaze upon the blaze. His sensibilities dulled as if he had entered a dream state, and an overwhelming sensation of drifting upward caused him to totter sideways, nearly dropping the artifact to the ground.

Billy! The master's shrill voice knifed through his brain, and dragged him back to the present.

The candle's power almost tricked him. In order to prevent it happening again, Billy wrapped his hand around the flame and was pleasantly surprised that there was no heat. But he still feared placing the magical tool in the bag with the other artifacts, so he gripped it with his left hand while using his right hand to grope toward the fourth and final obelisk.

Once again, as another of Jenny's magical tools was removed from its protective monument, the surrounding energy shifted but with more force this time. An earthquake rocked the graveyard, shoving tree roots and boulders out of the frozen earth. The shaking continued for several moments as Billy stumbled and collided with the tombstones. He feared the commotion would rouse the gnome and Guardian Crows from their forced slumber.

It was obvious to him that the hallowed ground was not pleased with his actions. The energy field's escalating response to each theft was disconcerting and left him wondering what catastrophic event would occur when he lifted the fourth artifact from its vault.

What am I doing? Billy thought. *I'm desecrating the final resting place of a powerful family. And for what? A greedy sorcerer who will cast me aside like unwanted garbage once he gets his hands on their extraordinary magical tools.*

Billy! the dark man yelled into his brain.

The hapless man abandoned his musings and lurched forward to complete his mission for the master. With his right hand stretched forward, he clutched the flame of truth in his left. Suddenly the toe of his boot snagged on a root and he slammed headlong into the fourth obelisk. Gripping his forehead, he rolled onto his back and groaned as rivulets of blood ran into his eyes and mouth. He gagged on the iron taste and spit gobs of bloody phlegm into the dirt.

During the collision, the perpetual flame of truth fell from Billy's grip and rolled behind a gravestone.

Clumsy oaf! Be quick! the dark master commanded.

Propelled into action by his master's sharp order, Billy staggered to his feet and began to unlock the secret symbols as he had done with the other three pillars. When the green flash appeared, the dark sorcerer directed him to quickly press the illuminated spot. Sitting inside the recess was a three-inch, silver-colored bell. Billy lifted it to his ear and shook it, but there was no sound.

No, don't shake the bell! the dark man screamed.

But it was too late. Believing the bell to be broken, Billy had already shaken it twice more.

Stop shaking the bell and put it in your bag now! You're summoning the elementals!

The most magical of Jenny's tools, the bell was crafted of various metals from the elemental families, and included iron, aluminum, brass, and silver. Its sole purpose was to summon the elemental spirits in times of great need.

Caaawwwww

Billy's sightless eyes frantically searched for the source of the sluggish sound in the branches of three ancient oak trees that loomed over the graveyard. Their limbs stretched low around the Seyler family plot in a protective embrace. Gazing through Billy's eyes, the master noticed a subtle movement.

Caaaawwwww

You fool! You summoned the Guardian Crows! Run before they catch and eat you!

In his current physical shape, the concept of running was not an option for Billy. His savaged body was not able to go faster than a drunken stumble and that's if he didn't catch his feet on any obstacles like headstones and the unforgiving tree roots.

Jenny's silver bell had deployed an emergency call to the elementals while also breaking the master's sleeping spell. Humans couldn't hear the soft angelic tone but, to nature's spirits, it rang out to them in one long melodious *Ohhhhmmmmmmm*.

Overhead, the Guardian Crows shook off their hazy disorientation. The gnome stretched and rubbed his eyes. Quickly scanning the scene, he saw the opened obelisks and Billy's leather pouch slung around his body. It didn't take long for him to arrive at a conclusion.

He pointed directly at Billy and yelled, "Stop the thief, he has stolen Jenny's magical tools!"

Panicked, Billy clutched his satchel and lumbered toward the exit. He tripped over John Seyler's foot stone and fell face to grave with John's epitaph. He scrambled to his feet and shuffled to the north gate where he bumped up against the wrought iron fence. Its pointy finials snatched his jacket in a vice grip.

"Help me!" Billy screamed as he yanked until the jacket ripped free from the fence. A tattered remnant fluttered in the breeze.

Get to the woods...now! The master's demand tore through Billy's frantic mind, and he lurched through the iron gate and staggered toward the Deep Woods as fast as he could. There was safety in the woods.

Caaaawwwww

The size of a pit bull, the massive crows launched into the air and scanned the cemetery for the intruder. Meanwhile, the gnome followed Billy and screamed updates as he trotted behind him. "He's heading for the Deep Woods. Get him!"

The dark man stood on the edge of the tree line. He dared not venture into the moonlight and resisted moving closer to the hallowed ground. The Seyler magic could still harm him. Even though Billy now possessed all of Jenny's ceremonial tools, the master needed them in his hands before he would feel safe.

Billy abruptly stopped.

"Master, I left the candle in the graveyard!" he cried out in a desperate voice. He glanced back toward the fourth obelisk. The brilliant blue flame flickered on the ground where Billy had dropped it.

Damn you! the dark man growled. *There's no time to go back. Come to me now!*

The gnome closed the distance on the sluggish intruder. "Come back thief!" he cried.

The Guardian Crows hovered overhead. A stream of magical energy—a beacon from Jenny's tools—snatched their attention.

"Help me, master!" Billy pleaded as he struggled toward the woods. Although he couldn't see them, he sensed the imminent danger from the Guardian Crows. To him, their presence felt like a blast of hot air.

The black birds cawed a battle cry to each other and dove toward their prey. With their eight-inch talons outstretched toward Billy, they closed the distance on the hapless man.

Winded, the gnome stopped and was content to watch the Guardian Crows finish the job.

"Help me!" Billy screamed.

Terrified, he tried to run but stumbled over his twisted feet and tumbled to the ground. The safety of the Deep Woods loomed only ten feet away but seemed like a mile as Billy clawed along the ground, one hand over the other, while the master waited in the shadows, his arm outstretched, his hand open and ready to snatch Billy when he got close enough.

Grab my hand, Billy. Grab my hand! the master yelled into Billy's mind.

Like an escaping lizard, Billy slithered back and forth on his belly as he wiggled toward the dark man.

The crows closed in. The downdraft from their wings buffeted Billy as he strained to reach for the sorcerer.

In one final effort, Billy launched himself forward just as a crow's talons sank deep into his shoulder bone.

Billy howled in agony. But his right hand had securely gripped the dark man and, in that same moment when their fingers touched, a brilliant white flash illuminated the sky. A booming thunderclap followed a split second later.

Billy and the dark man had vanished.

When they clasped hands, the master summoned his magic to escape into another dimension before the crows could grab Billy.

Well, before they could snatch *all* of him.

A Guardian Crow proudly strutted along the edge of the Deep Woods and displayed a trophy to his comrades. In his gigantic beak, dangled a grisly object oozing blood and gore. Although the crow had not captured the thief, it had managed to snatch the most important part of the grave robber. In its bill hung the severed shoulder and arm of Billy "The Tooth" Taylor. And wound around the amputated appendage was the leather pouch containing Jenny's stolen artifacts.

The Feather

Steven leaned against the granite boulder and brooded over his predicament. Despite the chilly weather, he sweated profusely. He wiped his forehead with the back of his sleeve and glanced up. Contrails streaked the blue winter sky with icy, white fingers.

It's going to freeze tonight, he thought.

Exhausted and pissed off, he spat angrily into the dirt. He had passed this same rocky ledge an hour earlier and now realized he had been hiking in circles.

Time was running out, and he needed a plan. The temperature continued to plummet, and he was poorly prepared—he had no water and wore only a thin windbreaker. He had planned for a quick thirty-minute walk in the woods to clear his mind. But now, the last light of the day raced over the mountains, and the chilled blast of a cold front buffeted him on his rocky perch.

He shook his head and moaned. Beth would know how to fix this. She had a cool head and knew exactly what to do.

Just be patient.

Beth's words tapped lightly on his brain. Steven was the antithesis of patience. He was a man of action—no time to plan, just get the job done.

Beth had patience to spare. Steven had once joked she should bottle her tranquil nature and sell it at a premium.

Don't worry, Steven. Just be patient and it will all work out.

He scowled. He missed her so much.

Beth lay in a coma, the tragic result of a drunken driver crashing into the front of her car while she had been stopped at a traffic light. The teenage driver had sailed through his windshield and tumbled into the street. The front of his car had launched toward Beth and pinned her against her seat, pushing the steering wheel into her chest.

After receiving a call from the police, Steven had raced to the scene and arrived just as the EMTs wheeled an unresponsive Beth into the ambulance amid a tangle of tubes and machine alerts. Steven's world had exploded and he wanted to scream or unleash his fury on something or someone. That's when he'd noticed a struggle next to the ambulance.

The drunk driver fought with the police and complained about the gash over his eye, his only injury. "Honest, she pulled in front of me. She ran the light."

Enraged, Steven lunged at the teenager. "You little prick!" he screamed.

That was six months ago. Beth remained in a coma and the belligerent teenager sat comfortably in the county jail.

Steven visited Beth daily. His hospital routine was their new normal: he read the news of the day, massaged her feet and legs, held her hand, and willed her to open her eyes. "Squeeze my hand, Beth. Just open your eyes."

Just be patient.

The morning of his hike, Beth's doctor entered the room. Her blank face provided no indication of the news to follow. "Beth's condition is getting worse," Dr. Pena began as she flipped a page on the chart. "Despite our efforts, her systems are shutting down. I suggest you prepare for the inevitable."

"What do you mean? We can't give up. I can't give up!"

Dr. Pena rambled off technical reasons why Beth would not survive, but Steven didn't hear her. Denial and regret consumed him as images filtered through his mind—memories of their happier moments and snapshots of future events without his wife.

Guilt pricked his heart.

As the doctor droned on, Steven's thoughts raced far away from the dreadful news. Sweat streamed down his face and his head pounded. The air in the room grew thick and oppressive, and he felt the walls closing in and suffocating him. He had to escape and get outside.

He fled to the top floor of the parking garage. The deserted deck opened up to the heavens, which swirled solemn and gray. He ran to the side and screamed into the ether. He sobbed uncontrollably as he cursed the world for Beth's situation.

Then he remembered the bench in the state park. A hand-carved block of granite sunk deep into the earth, the bench awaited visitors at the end of a beautiful, creek-side, nature trail. Nobody knew how it got there, or who had carefully etched symbols along the edge of the seat and down the solid stone legs, only that it had appeared almost fifty years ago. The unique bench had born witness to his courtship with Beth, where they had spent hours sitting in the shade of the oak trees, talking about their future together.

Steven desperately needed to talk with Beth now.

Thirty minutes later he pulled into the gravel parking lot. The familiar crunching sound as the tires drove over the gray rock tugged at sweet memories. He wasn't surprised to find the lot empty. After all, it was winter. Snow hadn't fallen yet, but the nights were freezing.

He grabbed his windbreaker and backpack and walked across the wooden bridge to the trailhead that led to the bench. Here was the juncture for two scenic paths: to the left, the short nature trail along the creek and straight ahead, the ten-mile loop into the mountains. Beth had once begged him to venture into the wilderness on the longer hike, but Steven had convinced her to take the short walk to the bench, their bench. Now, as he stood at the fork of the two trails, he wished he had taken her on the longer walk.

It would have made her happy.

Suddenly, a shriek pierced the air. Steven winced, knowing the sound was the desperate cry of an animal that had been mortally wounded. He scanned the woods and saw the blurred motion of a furry animal scampering away, carrying a tangled white mess in its jaws.

"Hey!" Steven yelled as he rushed to intercept the creature. Nearing the animal, he realized he was chasing a red fox. In its jaws hung a white crow almost the size of the fox itself. The bird was not dead and struggled to free itself, its injured wings flailing but inflicting no harm on its attacker.

Steven threw a rock, and it bounced in front of the fox. The animal stopped momentarily and glared at Steven. "Drop it!" he shouted as he sprinted toward the fox. The animal whirled and darted the other direction, dragging its squawking prey with it.

Steven scooped up a large branch and hurled it. It grazed the fox's head and the bird dropped to the ground. He immediately grabbed another branch and slung it sideways like a boomerang, hitting the animal in the side. "Go away. Get out of here!" Steven yelled as he waved his arms. The fox studied the attacking giant and then glanced at the hapless crow, which flopped on the ground. The fox chose to abandon its meal and barked insults as it darted into the underbrush.

Steven carefully approached. A rumpled mass of bloody white feathers lay still on the ground. He knelt. He could see the bird was alive, but barely. It shuddered and looked at him, its black eyes blinking slowly as if going to sleep. "Hi buddy," Steven soothed. "I won't hurt you."

He pulled an extra shirt from his backpack and carefully swaddled the bird to keep it warm. Like a newborn baby, the crow lay still in the crook of Steven's arm as he studied it. White corvids were rare in the area, and Steven investigated every detail of the shivering bird, marveling at its immense size and, despite the carnage, the beauty of its white plumage.

He could tell the bird would not survive. One wing was clearly broken and the other was almost detached. Blood oozed from its wounds and its nostrils. The fragile creature shivered and slowly shut its eyes. Steven cradled the dying crow and thought of Beth.

Please don't die.

A light winter breeze kicked leaves around the pair as the crow gently passed away. Steven blinked back tears as he tenderly stroked the bird's head and sobbed.

Steven wondered if the Fates had led him to this exact spot, to be part of this pitiful play. He wasn't a religious person, but Beth had enlightened him to the possibilities of powers stronger than himself. She taught him about the elements of nature, the spirits that influence all the physical realms on earth, and that all living things were connected and sacred.

The white crow was a warrior who had fought gallantly to keep its life, so Steven decided to honor the bird with a proper burial. Using a flat rock and his hands, he dug a shallow grave. He gently laid the body into the hole and scooped soil and leaves until he formed a small mound. To prevent scavengers from unearthing the body, he placed a large rock on top. He stood back and studied his work. Something was missing. He needed a marker for the courageous crow.

A feather—pure white with two tiny drops of blood on one side—lay on the ground where the fox had dropped the unfortunate bird. Steven picked it up and gently pushed it into the grave and bowed his head in reverence.

A large shadow swept over the ground, and Steven glanced up. A flock of crows flew overhead. One bird dropped out of the sky and landed on the grave in front of Steven. It cocked its head and stared at him, studying him, measuring his intentions. Steven remained quiet. He peered into the black eyes of the visitor who was predominantly black with a few feathers of white. He wondered if it was related to the poor creature buried in the ground. Abruptly the crow launched into the air and joined the others as they flew away calling to each other.

Exhausted and emotionally spent, Steven turned to leave. Then he realized something was amiss. He frantically scanned the area around him. Nothing was familiar. In his haste to save the white crow, he had run too far from the familiar nature trail. He was no longer near the creek and was in a large clearing framed by towering oak trees. *Don't panic. Take a deep breath.*

Just be patient.

Patience was not an option for Steven. His anxiety soared as he mentally calculated the odds of being permanently lost (or dying) in unfamiliar woods. He had told no one of his plans to visit the park. Panic controlled his legs, compelling him to bolt in the direction he thought would lead to the parking lot. He scrambled through bushes and swept branches aside as they ripped at his clothes. Running blindly, he tumbled hard to the ground when his feet snagged on rocks jutting out of the dirt.

The fall knocked his panic aside. He rolled onto his back and panted as he stared into the sky. *I've got to calm down.*

A flock of crows cawed as they flew overhead. He sat up and watched them disappear behind the tree canopy. *I've got to find the trail.* Steven stood and tested his ankles. Surprisingly there were no lingering effects of the fall. *That was lucky.*

Searching the forest for the trailhead, he spied a single-track path. He hurried down the dirt trail not realizing he was running higher up the mountainside, not going down toward the creek. It wasn't long before he found himself at the rocky ledge for the first time.

That was over two hours ago. Now, the azure sky had surrendered to a thick bank of winter clouds pregnant with rain and snow. Steven clenched the windbreaker around his body and scowled. *Damn, I wish I had brought my heavy coat.*

His anger rose easily on the wings of impatience. He kicked at the dirt and shouted into the valley, "Fuck!"

Just be patient.

Beth's words jerked him back to reality. Long shadows spread across the valley. It was twilight in the thickness of the forest. There wasn't much time to waste unless he wanted to endure a freezing night in the woods with no shelter and no water. Steven felt stupid and hopeless. He felt sorry for himself.

Just get on with it!

The words fluttered through his brain, prompting him to grin despite his situation. Beth had always talked to herself when confronted with a problem. If she began wallowing in self-pity, she would speak those words aloud, laugh, and get on with it.

Large snowflakes drifted onto his rocky sanctuary. *Time to get out of here and go home.*

He marched downhill. His spirits lightened as the pitch and smoothness of the path allowed him to trot. Just as he gained momentum, he encountered a fork in the trail and stopped. Two tracks led off into the brush. He absently bit his lower lip and chewed on his next decision. He was convinced he ventured right on his first foray into the woods, but the rocky trail had hidden all evidence of that earlier passage.

He closed his eyes, inhaled a deep breath, and whispered. "Beth, help me get out of this."

When he opened his eyes, something had changed. Three feet down the trail on the left, a white feather fluttered in the middle of the path. It wasn't there seconds ago. Steven slowly approached, glancing around to see if anybody or anything lurked nearby. He knelt down and picked up the feather. It looked like the one that he had reverently placed on the white crow's grave. He turned it over and saw two small drops of blood. *What the hell?*

CAW!

Steven looked up into the trees and saw a black bird fly away. He was confused. Was this some sort of crow magic? Was Beth orchestrating these events from her deathbed?

He looked down at the feather in his hand and instinctively nodded. Although he couldn't explain how it was happening, the crow, or Beth, was leading him out of the woods, and intended for him to follow the trail marked with the feather.

Steven knelt and jabbed the feather back into the ground. "I believe this belongs to you," he whispered as he gazed upward.

He gathered his belongings and quickly followed the dirt trail. To Steven's surprise, the path headed upward, back toward the rocky ledge. He panicked. To him *up* was bad and *down* was good. He stopped in his tracks. Immediately a loud caw hailed from above as a crow descended and flew several feet above the ground, paralleling the upward trail. For once in his life, he was going to be patient and pay attention to the natural signs around him. Suppressing his uncertainty, he pressed forward, trusting the crow.

That pathway soon gave way to a large clearing. Three trails spoked away from the grassy area, each path leading in a different direction. Steven couldn't remember which way to go and ran to each path, anxiously looking for any indication he had been there earlier, but saw nothing.

A sudden gust of frigid air punched through his thin layer of clothes. Goose pimples formed on his arms, and he hugged himself against the cold. Icy fingers tickled his spine as fear crept into his thoughts. *What if I don't make it out? I'll die here all alone.*

The morbid thoughts escalated his terror. His heart hammered and he panted. Panic poised at the tip of his brain. If he didn't do something right away to quell the mounting fear, he knew he would bolt in any direction, right or wrong.

Just be patient.

Beth's words drifted into his mind like a soft caress. Steven squeezed his eyes shut and imagined her standing in front of him holding his hands and smiling. "Help me, Beth, which way do I go?"

A welcoming warmth covered him, first beginning at his head and then melting down his skin to the soles of his feet. With his anxiety easing, he drew in a long breath and slowly exhaled. He opened his eyes. Ahead of him, down one of the pathways, appeared a white feather twirling in the winter breeze. Steven shook his head. *How is this happening?* He walked down the trail, knelt and picked up the feather. It was the same one as before, two dots of blood on one side.

CAW!

A murder of crows flew overhead.

As before, Steven placed the feather back into the ground and continued on the chosen path. The terrain sloped downward this time, buoying Steven's spirit. He quickened his pace, excited that he was finally travelling toward the creek and the gravel parking lot. He walked fast, and when the trail became level, he trotted. The path stopped at the water with a spur leading to the right and one to the left.

Once again, he was in unfamiliar territory.

Twilight claimed the forest with long, shadowy fingers, and the temperature plummeted. Steven needed to find his car soon. From above, the crows called out to him and urged him to trust his intuition.

Steven peered into the darkened sky. Although he couldn't see the black birds, he could sense their presence and understood what needed to be done. He closed his eyes. "Beth, help me get to the parking lot." And, he added, "Crows, please help me get to Beth."

When he opened his eyes, the familiar feather twisted at the entranceway to the trail on the left. Steven nodded and swiftly walked in that direction. The moss-covered pathway emerged into another clearing. This area was familiar. It was the final resting place of the white crow. Steven hurried to the gravesite and was surprised by the appearance of a huge crow perched on the large rock marking the grave. The plumage on this bird was mainly black except for flashes of white under each wing. In its beak fluttered the white feather. The crow jumped from its perch and gently poked the feather into the ground at the head of the grave. It cocked its head and peered at Steven.

CAW!

It launched into the air and flew several feet above the ground as it followed a rustic path. Steven chased after it. He trusted the bird would lead him out of the woods. Not far away he encountered the wooden bridge that led to the gravel parking lot. He hugged the railing as if it was a life preserver—his link to his safety and to Beth. He then glanced to the parking lot.

The crow perched on his car. It ruffled its feathers, clacked its bill, and soared off into the sky. Steven sprinted to his car, yanked the door opened, and hopped in. Cranking the engine, he turned the heater to high, and grabbed the blanket from the back seat. As the heat enveloped him like a warm cocoon, his shivering lessened.

He closed his eyes. *Thanks Beth. Thank you for sending the crows to help me.*

The window had fogged immediately when he turned on the heater, but as the windshield cleared, Steven noticed something fluttering on the glass outside. He cautiously exited the car, plucked the item from underneath the wiper, and carried it inside. The crow had left him one final gift—a black feather with white markings.

Using fishing line that he stowed in his glove box, Steven gently wound the filament around the quill several times before knotting it and creating a loop, which he tied around the rearview mirror. He leaned back in his seat and watched the feather pirouette in the heated air, flashing black and white until it blurred.

Steven's phone abruptly rang. He jerked at the sudden noise, anxiously looked at the number, and cringed. The hospital was calling and he feared the worst. "Hello?" He answered in a trembling voice.

"Mr. Davis?"

"Yes. Who's this?"

"Mr. Davis, this is Dr. Pena, your wife's doctor." Steven steeled himself for the bad news. "I don't know how this happened, Mr. Davis, but your wife, well, we just can't explain it..."

"Just say it!" Steven demanded.

"Mr. Davis, your wife woke up ten minutes ago and her vitals are strong. She's asking for you, and she keeps asking about the crows. Do you know what she might be talking about?"

The doctor's voice grew distant as Steven slowly lowered the phone to his lap. Relief washed over him and fear melted away. A peaceful calm engulfed him like a comforting hug, and he allowed himself to finally relax.

The feather hypnotically turned, twirling first to black and then flashing to white. He studied its movement as he mused above the day's events. One thing was clear. Beth *did* reach out to him. With the crows' assistance, she demonstrated the importance of patience and the value of faith, not only in one's self, but in others.

CAW!

Steven gazed at the sky splashed with the muted colors of the retreating day. A murder of crows soared overhead, and called out to him one last time.

Holding his hand over his heart, he followed their flight and sent one final message. *Thank you for uniting me with Beth.*

Eyes

This story was crafted from an idea submitted during a contest I held for my readers who voted on the submissions.

Congratulations, Andrea, for your story idea.

Remember me and learn from my mistakes.

It all began with an unusual weather event that drenched my town of Aningan. Five straight days of relentless rain pushed rivers over their banks and spawned mudslides, which swallowed roadways and neighborhoods. Many mountain communities were cut off as ancient trees toppled across access roads.

"Shelter in place!" The piercing order echoed up the mountain slope as a police cruiser maneuvered around fallen trees and notified residents of the dire situation. "Do not leave your home for any reason."

I slowed my car to a crawl as I approached the cruiser. The officer and I stared at each other as I inched by. I managed a weak smile, and then my stomach lurched as the officer motioned for me to stop.

I peered at him through slitted eyes as the window lowered and rain stung my cheeks.

"Sir, you shouldn't be out. Please go back home," he said as he shielded his eyes.

"Sure thing," I replied and turned away.

"Just a minute," the officer shouted. I froze. Bile jumped into my throat and I burped acid fumes. "That's a bad crack in your windshield. And, one of your wipers isn't working."

"A branch fell on the car." I hoped I sounded calm and nonchalant, but my insides were churning. I gulped and stared through the windshield like I was inspecting the crack, but I was avoiding his stare.

My eyes give me away. I'm a lousy poker player.

"That's too bad," he commiserated as he shined the cruiser's spotlight on the windshield. He lingered on the crack longer than I wanted, but I stared straight ahead and tapped my fingers on the steering wheel.

"Was that a big branch?"

His question startled me. A branch is a branch, isn't it? I separated my hands as I demonstrated the length of two feet. "But it was thick. It bounced off the glass and fell over to the side about a mile down the mountain."

The officer squinted at my demonstration. He nudged his service cap up and scratched his head.

He knew I was lying.

My hands were clammy on the steering wheel. Not from the rain, but from fear. My heart pounded, and my mouth went dry like every ounce of moisture had been wicked away. My fingers twitched toward the gearshift. If only I could shove the car into drive and mash the pedal. I'd be free.

What a shitty plan.

"Okay, sir. Move along and get back home. I'll stay in the neighborhood in case you need me.

I nodded at him and replied, "Stay safe." The window moved up and latched. I breathed a big sigh of relief that momentarily fogged the front window. I slowly inched forward as I kept a wary eye on the cruiser in my side mirror.

I was a car length away when the lights on the top of his car turned on. The eerie blue glare bathed the shadowy forests in an ominous glow.

"Shit," I hissed as I stopped.

The officer opened his door and stepped out. He held his flashlight at shoulder level and shined the light on my face as he walked toward my car. He rapped the window with his knuckles. I peered at him and moved the window down. I hoped I looked innocent.

Rain flew in but despite the wetness, my mouth was still dry as a desert. I licked my lips and asked, "Did you forget something?"

The flashlight blinded me as he walked by and inspected the crack. He flicked the light into my face and studied me before he returned to the windshield. "This crack is much bigger than a two-foot branch."

His words knifed into my gut and twisted.

I said nothing. What could I say? I didn't have a back-up plan.

My eyes darted to the officer, the windshield and my glove box where I kept my gun. My hands fell into my lap and twisted around each other as he strode in front my car and then around to the other side. The light burned guilt into my soul.

Then the officer reached for something on the window. I leaned forward and watched him. A chill raced up my spine. What did he see?

He extracted something thin from under the broken wiper blade. He sauntered to the driver's side as he held the item in his hand and studied it. "Looks like it was pine," he noted.

"Pine what?" I responded.

"A pine tree branch. Look, here's a twig with small cones. It was stuck under your wiper. And, there's something else."

My breath caught in my throat.

"There's a black feather snagged in the branch. Looks like a crow feather."

"Huh," I remarked. I clenched my jaws.

The officer looked at me again. "Might have been a crow nest in that pine. Do you want the feather?"

I was flustered by his interrogation and blurted, "Sure."

He passed the small sodden feather through the window and I pinched it between my thumb and forefinger. I studied it before stuffing it into my shirt pocket.

"Well, I better get going. I've got more houses to check." The officer dipped his hat and a trickle of water streamed in front of his face. He ambled back to his car, slid in and turned off the lights. I watched him pull off into the distance before I dared to move forward.

I was very late.

My friends were expecting me over an hour ago. The damned storm and my little 'incident' delayed me. I had my story prepared in case there were questions. I'd explain about the branch crashing onto my windshield, and add the officer's assertion that it must have been a pine tree. And, I would produce the crow's feather as additional evidence.

Yes. That sounds believable.

If I only I could convince myself.

Eyes floated in the darkness just in front of the car and I slammed on the brakes.

What the hell? I blinked and looked again.

Nothing

Get a grip, Robert. You're losing it man.

I mashed lightly on the accelerator. A flicker of lightning illuminated a woman standing in front of my bumper. I slammed on the brakes and stared out the windshield. The one working blade flopped back and forth as I peered through the glass between passes.

Nothing. Just the rain and the darkness.

Was that a ghost? I gripped the steering wheel and forced a scream down my throat.

I hadn't meant to hit her. The rain. The darkness. She was walking in the middle of the road.

The last thing I remember were her eyes—wide and fearful—just before I ran her over with the car. She flew onto the hood and crashed into the windshield before she tumbled over the side of the car. That split second before she fell to the side, we stared at each other. Her icy blue eyes stopped my heart. Strands of raven-black hair, slick from the rain, stuck to her pale face.

I may have been driving too fast.

I was late for Bill's Halloween party. Between the craziness at work, the incessant storm warnings, and my desire to have a much-needed weekend in the mountains, I was eager to get to Bill's home before nightfall.

Okay, I was speeding.

I fish-tailed some of the switchbacks as I drove up the slope. The radio squawked warnings that access to some mountain communities was limited due to the weather. I couldn't allow this stupid storm to ruin my weekend.

Nobody was going to take my vacation away from me.

But she almost did.

After striking her, I stayed in the car praying it wasn't actually a person. Maybe it was a deer. But deer don't have bright blue eyes, do they? The darkness and downpour made it impossible to see anything, so I knew I had to get out of the car.

I slid out and stood in the rain. Whatever I hit fell over the hood on the driver's side. I scanned the roadway. The blackness was suffocating. I shuffled my feet as I crept along trying to hug the asphalt and not step into the slick vegetation on the side. I didn't have a flashlight and didn't want to use my phone's light in the rain, so I tread lightly as I walked all around the vehicle.

Nothing.

I looked to the left. There was tall grass that spilled down a steep embankment. In this rain, if anything fell there, it would have plummeted downward like it was on a water slide. I glanced up the road and behind the car.

Nothing.

That's when I convinced myself it was a figment of my imagination. Never mind that the windshield had a huge crack down the middle. There was no evidence, and that means it didn't happen.

Right?

The rest of the drive was uneventful as I wound further up the mountain to the chalet at the top. A long weekend with friends who I hadn't seen for years seemed like the perfect way to spend a rainy forecast.

The chalet belonged to Bill. He was a chef at a local eatery, and I looked forward to his dinner. I hoped they hadn't started without me. I was starving. I had phoned, but in the mountain, cell service was sketchy.

The other folks expected for the weekend were Bill's fiancé, Phoebe, Janet and Susan, and Roger and Naomi. I was the odd person out, but I didn't care. Bill invited me to bring a friend, but I didn't have time for relationships. I was too busy. Hell, it had been years since I had chatted with any of my friends, so I looked forward to reconnecting.

I hadn't met Phoebe. Nobody had met Phoebe.

Bill planned a special party to surprise his fiancé. She loved surprises, and as a way to introduce her to his friends, he concocted a creepy Halloween gathering. "The party of a lifetime," he boasted on the phone. "You don't need a costume. Just come as you are."

I pulled into the driveway. *Great, they still have power.* Light shone through all the windows of the three-story chalet like a welcoming beacon in the gloomy night.

I dashed to the front door with my jacket hunched over my head and rang the bell. There was no answer so I pounded on the door. Bill finally answered. "I'm glad you could join us," he remarked, sarcasm tinging every word. "We're already on the fourth course, but I'm sure you can catch up."

He stood to the side as I passed through. I stomped the rain off my shoes and left my wet jacket on the hook in the foyer. "Come this way," he gestured.

I followed him into the dining room. Four pairs of eyes stared back at me. Four? I walked around the table hailing everyone: Janet. Susan. Roger. Naomi. We exchanged brief pleasantries before I whirled toward Bill. "Phoebe? Is Phoebe joining us?"

"Not just yet," he smirked. A twisted grin filled his face as he sat at the dining table. He gestured to the chair beside him. "Sit here, Robert." He pulled a bottle of chardonnay from the chiller and poured me a full glass. "You'll need this for tonight." Then he winked at me.

Everyone laughed.

I felt creeped out by that wink. I sipped the wine and stared at everyone over the rim. *What's so damned funny?*

"I'm glad you could join us, Robert," Susan mentioned as she lightly touched my hand. "We were worried you wouldn't come." Head nods and murmurs circled the table.

"Gee, I didn't realize my arrival was so important." I smiled and raised my glass. "To friends."

Eating, drinking and wonderful conversation filled the next hour. Robert brought us a potent dessert wine that paired exquisitely with his scrumptious apple tart. By the time dessert was consumed, I had forgotten about the police officer and the accident. I was drunk. I laughed and grinned at any comment. It had been too long since I'd been able to relax and unwind.

Bill lightly tapped the side of his goblet with his knife. "And, now, for the finale. Join me in the sitting room."

I collapsed into a stuffed chair near the massive stone fireplace. I gazed into the burning logs and my stomach flipped. The snapping of the burning wood propelled me back to the incident earlier that evening. I couldn't look away from the blaze. The flickering light had snatched my attention and was luring me toward it. Pulling me into it.

Her icy blue eyes floated in the orange glow.

"Robert?" Bill's voice yanked me back to reality.

I was no longer in the chair. I stood in front of the fireplace, dangerously close. His hand gripped my shoulder hard. "Are you okay? You almost walked right into the fire."

I nodded. "I'm okay. I was just admiring the stonework," I lied. I glared at the fire before returning to my chair.

"Attention, everyone," Bill announced. "This night is a special Halloween. You will finally meet my extraordinary fiancé, Phoebe. I lost her in a car accident a year ago."

Lost her in car accident? Phoebe's dead?

Bill pressed a remote and a large screen descended from the ceiling. All eyes were on Bill as he stood in front of the screen. "Phoebe adored surprises. What better way to introduce her to my incredible friends then by surprising all of you."

The lights went out as lightning stabbed a nearby tree. Thunder shook the house.

I gripped the arms of my chair and peered around the room. Black shadows danced in the darkness, illuminated only by the yellow glow of the fireplace.

A video flickered to life on the screen, and I jerked from the sudden noise. I glanced around the room. Bill stared back at me with a thin smile on his face. So did Susan, Janet, Roger, and Naomi.

"And, now, meet my Phoebe," Bill whispered.

A young girl drifted onto the screen. In a series of frames, her image faded in and out as she crept closer toward the camera. At first, she stood in the distant shadows of a forest and then with each pulse of the film, she appeared closer until her face filled the entire screen. Her slick, black hair clung to her white face as she grinned. Her icy-blue eyes drilled into my soul.

The dark-haired, blue-eyed beauty on the screen couldn't be the same girl I encountered down the mountain. Could she?

Bill's voice shattered the intensity of the moment. "Phoebe would like to get to know someone better." He gazed at her image with profound love in his eyes. "She left a token with one of you earlier this evening."

Bill glanced in my direction.

"Check your pockets. Does anyone possess a crow's feather?"

A breath hitched in my throat. *A crow's feather?*

"Anyone?"

"I have one," I squeaked.

A wide smile filled Bill's face. In the flickering orange glow of the fire, he looked remarkably like Dante as he stood in hell.

"Excellent. Let's see it," Bill insisted.

I pulled the feather out of my pocket and held it up. It was bedraggled from the soaking rain and from being stuffed in my shirt.

My friends circled around me and inspected it. They nodded approvingly and looked toward Bill.

Bill gestured for me to rise. "Robert. You're the chosen one tonight. Phoebe would like to surprise you."

"Wait a minute. How can I meet a dead person?" I asked while glancing around the room. My anxiousness was met with impassive stares.

"Join me, Robert." Bill wrapped his arm around my shoulders and pulled me in front of the screen. I glanced up. The young woman smiled back with a dark, creepy grin. Cold fingers of fear stroked my spine. It was the same look on the girl before she fell over the side of my car. "Show Phoebe your feather."

I pushed it toward the screen. Fear had seized my movements and the feather shook violently in the ghostly light.

Phoebe opened her mouth wide and screamed an unnatural, ear-splitting noise that shattered the mirrors and wine glasses. I dropped the feather and clamped my hands over my ears. Despite my intense feeling of dread, I couldn't prevent myself from staring at her image twisting and morphing. Her grotesque mouth had enlarged so much it now filled the entire screen, and her deafening screech echoed off the walls.

The room went black.

An urgency to flee poked at my brain, and I turned to leave. But where was the exit? Suffocating darkness and an eerie silence swirled around me as I crept to what I thought was the front door. Waving my arms back and forth in front of me, I suddenly struck something. Although solid, the object was soft and pliable like it may have been a person.

"Hello?" I whimpered, hoping nobody would answer.

My hammering heart and quickening breaths betrayed the terror building inside. My instincts screamed warnings to run, to get away.

A strong hand gripped my shoulder, and the bony fingers quickly burrowed into my muscles and directly to the bone.

I screamed and collapsed on the floor.

I don't know how long I had passed out but when I awoke, I was on my back and stared up into my friends' faces. The lights had come back on, and they all stood around me, peering at me with devilish grins.

"What happened?" I squeaked. *Wait. That wasn't my voice.*

Bill and Roger each grabbed an arm and lifted me up. They steadied me as I got my bearings. I must still be drunk because the room was spinning and nothing made sense. I took a step and lurched against Bill. He grabbed me around the waist. "Take it easy. You'll feel better soon," he reassured me.

"I feel strange," I whispered. Actually, I didn't feel like myself at all. An air of confusion swirled. I couldn't quite put my finger on it, but things were not as they used to be. I searched Bill's face. "What happened?"

There was that foreign voice again.

He smiled at me. A warm, loving smile like the one he had shown Phoebe when she first appeared on the screen. He guided me to the chair by the fireplace. "Sit down and relax."

I eased into the chair and tilted my head back against the upholstery. "How do you feel?" Susan asked as she lightly touched my hand.

"Odd. Very odd." The words were mine but the voice was not. I scrunched my face, confused by what was happening. "Something happened..." I stopped speaking. The tone was several octaves higher.

Did I hurt my throat when I fell to the floor?

"Look at this. It will help," Bill soothed. He offered me a hand mirror.

I resisted. "Why do I need that?" I coughed and cleared my throat hoping to remove whatever was affecting my voice.

"Trust me," Bill replied as he pushed the mirror toward me. He flashed his warm smile again.

Something was wrong. But I took the mirror from Bill anyway. My gaze focused on my lap while I slowly raised the mirror until it was in front of my face. I didn't want to look up, my instinct cautioned me against that action, but I had to. I needed to.

I searched my reflection. Shadows danced across my face in the fire's flickering orange glow. My heart raced with fear. And, yet, there was another side of me whose spirits soared with joy as I studied the long black hair and bright-blue eyes staring back. I glanced at Bill, my eyes full of questions.

He smiled. "It worked Phoebe. Your magic worked." He knelt beside me and wrapped his hand around mine. His touch felt so warm and comforting.

"I don't feel like me...yet." The voice was much higher and it startled me.

What was happening to me?

"Give it a little more time. Soon, there will be no more traces of Robert. Only you." Bill leaned forward and cradled my cheek with his hand.

"Very soon," Phoebe replied with my mouth.

The sickening reality filled me with dread. Phoebe's soul had somehow transferred into my body, and her magic was slowly eroding all remnants of my physical and mental identity.

I'm slipping away with each passing minute.

The Crystal Ball

The crystal ball sat alone on a metal table under the glare of the midday sun. Whenever the clouds passed overhead, dazzling colors skimmed across its reflective surface and flicked between hues of reds and blues. An intricately carved mahogany base cradled the six-inch orb like gnarled wooden fingers holding a delicate egg.

Unlike other trinkets and treasures displayed at the flea market, this object had been placed far away from the other vendor tables and almost into the parking lot. After several complaints were received, the market manager had no choice but to direct Jacob Charles to move his sphere at least ten feet away from everyone else.

Some people grumbled about the orb's disgusting smell. Others moaned about its constant ear-piercing squeal. But they all agreed that an overwhelming feeling of pure evil emanated from the unassuming shiny ball.

Jacob couldn't blame them.

He had lived with the cursed orb for only six months and couldn't stand to be near it. He loathed it and blamed the ball for his failing health.

He hunched in his camping chair under an immense golf umbrella. Mirrored sunglasses perched on the end of his sharp angular nose, and he wore a lopsided sneer that cracked wrinkles in his leathery cheeks. He reached into his duffel bag and discreetly withdrew a vodka nips. Holding the bottle in his lap he eyed passersby while he twisted the cap. Then he quickly poured the contents into his blue sports bottle. He took a swig, smacked his lips, and settled into the chair.

Despite the low price of two dollars, the sphere attracted little interest. On one occasion, three souls ventured closer to find out why the lonely item sat abandoned in the sun. But as if they had encountered a foul-smelling odor, they quickly turned back with disgusted grimaces etched on their faces.

Whenever a curious person showed an interest, Jacob would tense with hopefulness, his hand gripping the sports bottle in anticipation of a sale. But every time the potential buyer hurried away, that familiar feeling of disappointment squeezed his heart and he'd gasp as if a little bit of his life had been sucked away. He scanned the throng of eager shoppers quickly passing him. Their faces bore scowls of urgency, and Jacob wondered if they instinctively knew they were in the vicinity of something wicked.

Damned crystal ball, he thought. The words had barely flitted through his brain when a pain exploded in his stomach causing him to double over. During the episode, his hand involuntarily clenched the sports bottle so tightly the pressure propelled the cap five feet away.

"I'm sorry. I'm sorry," he hissed through clenched teeth. After an agonizing minute, the burning ache mysteriously disappeared.

He glared at the crystal ball but kept his mind blank. He didn't want another attack.

As the hours passed, the heat of his resentment rivaled the soaring summer temperature. *I've got to find a buyer.* He chose his words carefully to avoid the punishment that had been meted on him since he found the orb in January, six months earlier.

His first encounter with the crystal ball was when he moved to escape some incidents in his Georgia hometown. Bad luck followed him like gum on his shoe, and hard luck stories and "wrong place, wrong time" encounters plagued him. When he crossed the border into Florida, a thunderstorm had just passed through leaving the air freshly scrubbed clean and painting the sky with a beautifully arced rainbow. His mood lightened, and he smiled. He hadn't been happy in a long time, and he was convinced nature had sent him a sign that all would be okay.

A friend had connected him with a landlord who owned several tiny cabins for rent on the edge of town. In their previous life, the cabins had been part of a larger complex called Sleepy Haven Campground, which provided rustic lodging for travelers looking for a comfortable place to stay as they explored Florida's tourist sites. That was decades ago. The swamp reclaimed most of the campground, and the new owner bulldozed all the cabins except the seven that paralleled the road into town. Those he converted into weekly rentals.

Jacob lucked into an end unit. The one-room building had everything he needed to survive: a bed and chair, an end table, and a tiny fridge and stove. A convenience house located behind the cabins addressed his bathroom needs. There was no cable or internet, but another tenant possessed a portable radio and didn't mind sharing with the other renters on those Saturday nights when they'd hang around a picnic table and drink.

One day, as Jacob walked the three miles into town to pick up a few groceries (namely vodka, hot dogs, and potato chips), he passed a heap of items dumped on the edge of the road. Several feet back stood the charred remains of a clapboard house. The roof and three of the walls had caved in, but the red-brick fireplace jutted into the sky like a bloody spine.

He surveyed the mound of junked items and wrinkled his nose. They all smelled of smoke and most were charred, but one item appeared perfect and unscathed: a crystal ball and its carved mahogany stand. The orb sat on the top of the pile like a beacon.

Come to me.

It called to him with a melodic voice not unlike a tingling bell. He squinted at the orb, unsure of what he'd heard.

Come to me. Now!

It beckoned again, louder and more urgent. He glanced up into the cloudless sky. Although wintertime, the Florida sun baked his skin. *I'm imagining things,* he told himself. *I've got heat stroke or something.*

You're an idiot!

The unknown voice screamed in Jacob's brain and he flinched as though he had been slapped hard across the face. He rubbed his cheek and stared at the crystal ball. It pulsed and shimmered as rainbows skipped across its surface, mesmerizing...hypnotizing.

Jacob awoke hours later in his cabin. He sat on the edge of the bed and raked his fingers through his greasy hair, trying to rub consciousness back into his brain. Nothing made sense. *What day is it? How did I get here?*

A gentle tinkling drew his attention to the end table.

A chill of horror raced down his spine as he stared wide-eyed at the crystal ball.

Bile burned the back of his throat, and he gently rubbed his stomach which threatened to release the vomit boiling within it.

Hello, Jacob.

Jacob jerked at the cloying greeting that drifted through his mind. He scanned the tiny room. He was alone. Just him and the mysterious orb.

Today is your lucky day, Jacob. I will change your future.

"What?" Jacob whispered. He squeezed his eyes shut and then reopened them hoping the ball would be gone. It sat on the table, silent. A sudden ray of sunshine glinted off the surface, and a spear of light stabbed Jacob's right eye. He winced and turned away. Cautiously, he looked back at the sphere.

Mind me, Jacob, or I can make the pain worse.

"Who are you?" Jacob squeaked in a timid, childlike voice. "What do you want?"

You may call me Brom. I am all that you will ever need, and you will do my bidding from this day forward, or you will suffer the consequences.

Jacob was thirty-five when he was pressed into service by the mysterious crystal ball. After six cruel months in the cursed relationship, his humped back, wrinkled skin, and sunken eyes gave him the appearance of an ancient man on the verge of dying.

The orb was right about one thing. Jacob was never in need or want from that point forward. The sphere provided anything he imagined: money, food, and even whores. But they were only payment for the vile duties Jacob was forced to perform.

Crystal balls are well known for their ability to peer into the future and are seen as harmless divination tools. Brom's particular twist on this benign ability was knowing where and when deaths would occur, particularly the demise of unpleasant souls who already walked the earth with one leg in the dark pit of hell. These souls were the sweetest-tasting and Brom wanted them all for himself.

But they didn't always die as planned.

That's when Jacob was obligated to intervene.

After months of killing strangers (and almost being killed himself), his heart tired of the bloodshed. He may have been a bad-luck scoundrel for the majority of his life, but his tattered soul begged for mercy and for a much-needed change.

When he approached Brom about retiring from his responsibilities, the evil orb punished him so severely that Jacob lay unconscious for three days. Of course, Brom had seen this coming, but Jacob's insolence still infuriated him. *How dare he yearn to leave me.*

During the time Jacob wasn't able to carry Brom to feast on murderous souls, the sinister sphere reconsidered the request. After all, Jacob was near death anyway. So, when Jacob finally emerged from unconsciousness, Brom granted his wish to be free of their arrangement.

On one condition.

Jacob must find a suitable replacement.

And Brom knew where to go. *Go to the flea market this Saturday. Place me in the middle of a metal table away from everything else. Then sit and wait. My new companion will arrive in the afternoon. When she approaches you, do not try to dissuade her from her purchase.* Brom's last statement coiled through Jacob's brain like a spine-covered snake.

A painful migraine throbbed in his temples. He grabbed his head and nodded. "I understand, Brom. I won't interfere."

The afternoon shadows stretched long across the flea market parking lot. Sweat coursed down Jacob's face, a result of fear and not from the hot sun. Jacob was terrified that his replacement wouldn't show as expected. He couldn't bear another moment with Brom. He just couldn't.

A man exited the building and approached him. "Hiya, Jacob. You been sitting here all day?"

Jacob dipped his sunglasses and stared back with bloodshot eyes. "Yeah." The word rolled off his tongue slow and tired.

The man glanced at the crystal ball. "Why did you shove it in the sun. Ain't nobody gonna touch that hot piece of shit."

"It just takes one." Jacob was a man of few words.

The man gazed at Jacob and then back to the orb. With the sun lower in the sky, the iridescent colors in the sphere were easier to see...and appreciate. "Whatever, Jacob. I'm tired and I'm heading home."

Jacob watched his friend leave. His jaw muscles bunched and his teeth gnashed in frustration. "Gotta find that damned buyer," he hissed through clenched teeth.

A sudden movement caught his eye. As shoppers exited the flea market, a young woman walked by the table, stopped, and then took several steps backward. She chewed her lower lip as she stared at the lonely item sitting in the middle of the table. Then she cocked her head and took a tentative step forward.

Jacob held his breath and nervously scrutinized her every move.

Folding her arms, the woman slowly circled the table while maintaining her gaze on the sphere.

Jacob gripped the arms of his chair. The young woman hadn't bolted in disgust. She might be his replacement. He whipped off his sunglasses and peered at her, willing her to pick up the item. *Come on...pick it up.*

She took another step and another until she stood at the edge of the table. The fingers of her right hand twitched. Then, slowly, she extended an index finger toward the shiny ball.

Jacob's fingers nervously tapped the arm of his chair.

The young woman lifted the price tag and smiled before she carefully scooped up the ball and base. She tucked the orb in the crook of her elbow and turned around looking for the seller.

"Ain't that ball blistering hot?" Jacob asked as he approached her.

"This ball? No, not at all. Here, touch it," she said as she held the sphere toward him.

He stepped back and held his hands up. "Nope. That's okay. You lookin' to buy?"

"Is it really only two dollars?"

"Sure is. It's a bargain, ain't it?"

"It's the most beautiful thing I've ever seen." She said as she handed him a five-dollar bill. "Keep the change. This is worth much more." Then she lowered her head and drew closer to Jacob as she whispered, "You may think I'm crazy, but I could swear I heard this ball talking to me. That's why I stopped. I heard someone call my name."

The memory of his first encounter with Brom flashed through Jacob's brain. For a quick second he considered warning the young woman. She seemed so innocent, so full of life. But a kick inside his stomach reminded him that he had one last duty to perform before he would be free of the evil orb.

"Then I guess it was meant to be," he offered with a half grin. "Do you need a bag for it?"

"Oh, no. I don't want to cover up it's beauty," she cooed as she lovingly stroked the glassy surface and watched the dazzling colors swirl.

Jacob averted his eyes from Brom's mesmerizing magic.

Abruptly the woman stopped caressing the sphere and looked up. He shuddered. A white membrane covered her pale blue eyes, and the large pupils fixed their stare directly at him. Jacob knew it was Brom who now glared at him, and the young woman had been silenced for the time being.

Terror sucked the spit from Jacob's mouth, and he gagged on the dryness.

It's been fun, Jacob. But I must take my leave of you.

Jacob hacked as he desperately searched for something to quench his thirst. His blue sports bottle lay under his chair only six feet away. He clawed at his throat, coughing and choking, as he staggered to his chair. When he retrieved the bottle, it was empty.

There was one tiny thing I forgot to mention. Brom's irritating words drilled into Jacob's brain like an ice pick.

Gasping for air, Jacob collapsed onto the ground and reached toward Brom. "Water...I need...water."

Yes, I know you do. That's what I omitted from our little agreement. As you are aware, I always know when and where the blood-thirsty souls will die.

Jacob rolled onto his back as his black, swollen tongue pushed out of his mouth.

Well, Jacob, for the last six months what have you been doing for me? Brom chuckled. The sound rolled across Jacob's brain like the snarl of a hellhound. *That's right. You've been killing.*

Jacob's lungs jerked to suck in air. His wide, terrified eyes stared up at the young woman who looked down upon him with a devilish sneer and coal-black eyes.

So, I'm here to collect your delicious soul. Your demise is imminent. I can hear the death rattle racing upward. I can see your oxygen-starved heart and brain quiver.

You, my friend, are dead.

Jacob ceased gasping. A purplish-blue tinge formed around his eyes and neck as though he had been strangled by unseen hands.

Such a shame, Jacob. But it was certainly fun for me while it lasted. Now, Mia and I have places to go and souls to snatch.

The young woman cradled the crystal ball in her arms and exited the flea market.

Mia, let me explain how I will change your future, Brom instructed in his tinkling melodic voice.

The Harbinger

S usan huddled on the front porch and shivered. The first chill of fall arrived on a steady breeze that scrambled orange leaves across the front yard. She tightened her grip on a large pink blanket, a ragged remnant from her youth. Fuzzy slippers, the color of bubble gum, swallowed her feet.

CAW.

Susan shifted her gaze to the nearby cornfield full of broken and neglected stalks. A lone black crow sat on the fence post and watched her.

"Harbingers of death," her grandmother had warned her when she was six. "Steer clear of them. If they call for you, don't answer. For, if you do, they will lead you to your grave."

CAW.

The crow fluffed its feathers and screeched. The moment Susan peered at the bird, a shaft of sunlight stabbed through the gray storm clouds and bathed the crow in a dazzling light. Its iridescent plumage gleamed purples, blacks, and blues.

I wonder if grandmother was right, Susan thought as she studied the crow. *He seems harmless.*

Running a hand through her long hair, Susan's fingers absently traced the line of an old scar arcing across her scalp. An uneasy feeling rippled through her soul. She couldn't remember how long she'd been sitting on the porch, but her hands ached from the cold, and she instinctively curled her fingers deeper into the blanket.

Susan still lived in the house in which she was born. The frame home seemed much bigger in her childhood. Now the one-room dwelling appeared more like a ramshackle outbuilding that housed dusty reminders from years past. Wooden planks that were haphazardly nailed across the two windows did little to keep the elements outside. A round metal stack poked through black tar paper peeling away from the slanted roof. The sagging porch beckoned visitors into its gaping mouth—an off-kilter door that hung precariously by one hinge.

I should fix that door, she thought. *Dad wouldn't have let the house get so rundown.*

She missed her father. He was always fixing something. He especially loved tinkering on the family's ancient Chevy station wagon known as Old Blue. Faux-wood panels peeled away from each side of the powder-blue, rusted chassis, but the engine was sound thanks to Dad's magical hands. As a little girl, Susan had imagined the mechanical relic was her magical carriage that would carry her into town on special occasions where she could see other people and leave the isolation of the mountains behind.

Those rare excursions kept her sane and grounded.

CAW.

Shaken from her reverie, Susan followed the sound. The crow had flown past the porch to a nearby tree. It squawked and stared at her with beady black eyes.

Old Blue was now gone, destroyed in the crash that killed her parents ten years ago. She had survived the accident, barely. The car had skidded on black ice just before Haines Bridge. Dad had fought the steering wheel but eventually lost control as the car slammed sideways into the bridge and then pitched over the railing into the river below.

Mom and Dad had died instantly.

Susan had awakened amid the boulders on the water's edge. Blood streamed down her face. When she touched her head, she felt something soft and squishy. A chunk of her scalp had peeled away and felt foreign in her hands. She remembered feeling astonished that there was no pain but reasoned she was in shock.

Only tattered fragments remained of the accident. Each time she tried to recall the incident, she remembered less and less like ashes scattering in the wind. There were no recollections on how she got out of the river or if she even went to a hospital. She knew her parents were buried on the hill near the old oak tree because she had seen the granite stone that marked their graves. But she had no idea who provided the gravestone or who buried them.

Oftentimes, she would squeeze her eyes shut and focus hard on that cold autumn day she said goodbye to her parents. But the only detail that stepped forward was that she was all alone.

CAW.

The insistent crow demanded her attention.

Susan blinked several times to chase the daydream cobwebs away. That uneasy feeling returned as the crow perched on the porch railing and glared at her. It stretched toward her, and she instinctively leaned forward to meet it as though she understood it had a message to share. The pair stared into each other's eyes for several moments until a disquieting sensation crept up Susan's spine.

She wanted to bolt.

She needed to get away from the crow.

Sensing her decision to escape, the bird launched into the air like a black leaf rising in the fall breeze. It soared high and then dove low, gliding over the meadow behind the house and toward the oak tree. Toward the gravestone.

Susan followed the bird's flight path and trembled. Its movements sparked a recollection that had been hidden, no, thrust into the deep recesses of her brain. The crow's actions were familiar, something she'd witnessed before.

She didn't want to remember. It hurt too much.

CAW!

The black bird sat at the top of the tree and called to her like he had done many times since the car accident.

Fragments of a suppressed memory flashed in her mind like scattered pieces of a puzzle, except one piece was missing—herself. Although terror squeezed her insides, Susan knew what she must do.

Hugging the blanket, she rose and carefully navigated the rickety wooden steps spilling onto the front yard. Then she willed herself to walk toward the old oak tree. The crow circled overhead cawing encouragement.

With each step, another recollection materialized. Calm replaced her fear as she neared the tree, and she was ready to face the unknown, to confront the next phase of her existence.

When she reached the oak, she gazed up at the black bird. She now understood why he'd been pressing her to visit this place.

CAW.

It dropped to a lower branch and clacked its bill. Her eyes widened as dozens of crows joined their companion and filled the tree like a flush of ebony leaves. One large corvid flew to a nearby stone and cawed at her.

Susan took several hesitant steps forward.

Horrifying images flooded her brain as the last piece of the puzzle fell into place. Pain wracked the side of her head and she grabbed at the scar. When she pulled her hand away, blood pooled in her palm.

"I'm afraid," she cried out. She wanted to run away like she always did.

Keep running. The grave isn't real if you don't see it, she had told herself countless times before.

The murder of crows took to the air and encircled her like a black tornado. Squawks and screeches filled the air, and Susan clamped her hands over her ears to drown out the deafening noise.

"Stop!" she screamed.

Caw. Caw. CAW!

Silence.

Susan's eyes fluttered open. It was eerily quiet and calm. The birds had disappeared, and she had fallen onto her knees in front of the headstone. She forced herself to glance up and read the marker. As she mouthed the words, she ran her fingers over the rough granite surface and traced the engraved letters.

Here Lies a Loving Family
William, Martha and their daughter Susan
Entered Heaven Together Oct. 1, 1965

An Easy Mark

This story was crafted from an idea submitted during a contest I held for my readers who voted on the submissions.

Congratulations, Melodye, for a great idea.

"Worth every penny," the gray-haired man proclaimed. He leaned toward his companion, a young man with dark brown hair, and continued the conversation in hushed tones as his eyes darted around the dining room. After delivering his message, he snapped his fingers at the waiter. "Another bottle of Cabernet, please."

"Fascinating. And he talks to you?" the young man asked.

"Shh! Discretion is the utmost importance. Speak low."

"My apologies, father. I forgot."

Travis Tinker sat at the nearby table and stretched his ear toward the two gentlemen. The word discretion snatched his attention.

That term was typically used by those wishing to keep a secret. And, secrets usually involved something of value.

The restaurant buzzed with lunchtime activity so Travis couldn't hear the entire conversation, but his ears twitched at the words *dead*, *gold*, and *rich*. A grin creased his tanned face and his eyes danced with delight. He sensed an opportunity.

"Sir, what would you like to drink?"

Engrossed in eavesdropping, Travis didn't hear the waiter's question.

"Sir, what would you like to drink?" the server repeated in a louder tone as he scowled at Travis' unusual behavior.

Travis turned in his chair and flashed a quick smile before grabbing the drink list and running his finger down the wines. He huffed and slammed the list to the table. "You don't have what I want. Just bring me water for now."

The waiter's lips thinned and his eyes squinted with an air of suspicion as he examined Travis' clothes. His dark brown suit coat was a shade darker than his beige dress pants. The coat buttons were mismatched and frayed threads fluttered where the last button should have been fastened. Tavis fidgeted with the neon blue tie at his throat. The garish paisley tie was the easiest one to nick from the haberdasher store around the corner.

"Will you be dining, sir?" The waiter arched an eyebrow.

"You're conduct is putting me off my food, so we'll see. Just bring me my water for now," Travis said in his most authoritative voice as he dismissed the waiter with a wave of his hand. The server turned on his heel and marched away.

Travis fingered the change in his pocket. He didn't even have enough money to buy the bread sitting in front of him, much less dinner. But he didn't come to the upscale restaurant to eat. He came to find an easy mark. He glanced sideways at the two gentlemen and grinned.

Travis studied his targets. Age spots peppered the forehead of the gray-haired man. *Probably seventy,* Travis thought. His thinning gray hair was oiled and combed back in thin rows as though his scalp had been freshly tilled. He wore a slate-gray pinstripe suit and bright white shirt. A blood-red tie spilled down the front. A trimmed gray mustache splashed his upper lip while a patch of white hair smudged his chin in a finely trimmed goatee. His demeanor was one of control and good upbringing. He commanded the wait staff with a effortless mix of confidence and arrogance.

His companion possessed thick brown hair and broad shoulders. He wore a dark blue suit, light blue shirt, and a navy and red striped tie. A gold crest was embroidered above his left breast but Travis couldn't make out the details. *College? Father and son?*

The waiter only talked to the older man, but respectively nodded at the younger man, acknowledging his importance. The two men ordered steaks but the old man ordered the after-dinner brandy for both of them. All the interesting minutia traveled through Travis' brain like ticker tape, secured in his memory for retrieval at a later date.

"Sir, your water." Travis peered up at the waiter's scowling face. "Thank you."

"Would you care to order dinner?"

Travis grabbed a slice of bread from the basket and buttered it before answering. "I'm still considering my options."

The waiter didn't leave and the two men stared at each other.

"That's all for now," Travis said with a flick of his hand. The server stormed off.

"I have an appointment to see him tomorrow. You could go instead," the elderly man whispered.

Travis dropped his napkin on the floor and discreetly leaned toward their table.

"Is that allowed?" the young man asked in a confidential tone.

The old man chuckled. "Yes, they do have specific rules that must be adhered to." The old man stopped and glanced around the room. "Discretion is important. Let's go to the balcony and continue our conversation." The old man gestured to the waiter. "Paul, we're having a smoke. We'll be back in ten minutes."

"Yes sir, Mr. Randall. When you return, I'll freshen your drinks."

The old man nodded and smiled. He discreetly handed something to the server who palmed it and dipped his head. The two gentlemen disappeared through the French doors that led to the balcony. Travis watched them exit. The younger man was his height and had the same hair color. The older man stood almost six-foot tall and carried himself like he had been in the military.

Travis hailed his waiter.

"Yes sir. Are you ready to order?"

"Not just yet."

"What a surprise."

"I want to smoke a cigar before dinner. Where should I go?" They waiter stared at him for several moments before gesturing toward the balcony. "Feel free to exit those doors to smoke. I'll ensure your table is not disturbed." The server glanced at the water glass and quickly left.

Travis rose and strode confidently toward the French doors. He inhaled a deep breath and headed outside. A smoky haze encircled five men smoking cigars and brown cigarettes. Mr. Randall and his son stood by the far end of the balcony near a large tropical plant. Travis maneuvered to that area making small talk with each person he passed.

He glanced at his marks. They were deep in conversation and didn't notice him sidle up on the other side of the giant bird of paradise.

"Jonathan, as I mentioned before, you must be very careful how you handle these matters." The old man sucked on his cigar and blew the smoke into the air. "The visits cost one million dollars each, so each visit must be carefully crafted to maximize your ROI. Ask the right questions, stick to the script, and don't waste time."

"I understand, Dad. But it seems a little creepy talking to a dead person. Especially, my grandfather."

The old man chuckled. "G-pop was just as frugal with his money as I am." The old man signed a cross on his chest. "God rest his soul."

"But why him? Why are you paying so much money to visit him?"

"The gold bullion."

Travis' ears twitched. *Gold bullion.*

"G-pop was a shrewd business man, but he also possessed a nefarious side. He came from humble beginnings and made his riches dealing with the faceless people of the night—those who would do anything for a dollar."

"G-pop was a gangster?" the young man asked as he puffed his cigar and coughed.

The old man chuckled. "No, son, he wasn't a gangster, but he was well-respected just as much by the street people as he was by his business associates."

The old man stopped. After two puffs on his cigar, he continued.

"Back in 1954, he and three of his cronies robbed an armored truck carrying gold."

"What?" The tone of the young man's voice raised with surprise, and the old man held his hand up to quiet him.

"Shh. We don't need to announce family secrets, do we?" He flashed a sinister smile that made Travis cringe. "The gang buried the gold and planned to lay low for twenty years. That's a long time for a man to be patient with billions of dollars teasing him every minute of every day." The old man puffed his cigar and glanced over the city where lights twinkled in the twilight.

"Where did they bury it?" The young man asked in a barely audible tone.

"That's a good question. G-pop's been stubborn to share that detail. What I do know is that the gold is buried in a safe inside a mountain cave. An old mine shaft I believe. The lock requires four keys, one key from each conspirator." He blew smoke rings into the air. "Funny thing. Everyone passed away the same year as the robbery. I wonder if the gold is cursed."

"If everyone is dead, then you'll never be able to find the gold. There are no keys." The young man puffed his cigar and coughed.

"Logical. However, according to G-pop, the gang forged an agreement that all the keys would be kept with an agent, a lawyer unknown to all the perpetrators of the crime. This lawyer would hold the box containing the keys until the appropriate date when he would contact everyone to retrieve them."

"Appropriate date? When is that?"

"G-pop told me that the date they all agreed to was April 1, 1974." The old man grinned and shook his head. "Your grandfather had a unique sense of humor."

"But, that's this weekend. Only three days away."

The old man poked his cigar at his son. "Exactly. The solicitor has already sent out the notices. As executor of my father's estate, I received that letter. It specifically says that only the individuals named in the letter may arrive at his office and must provide the code word. The details of the agreement state that the keys will be distributed to the surviving members. If there are no survivors, then next of kin will be considered if they can provide the code word."

"Did G-pop divulge the code word?" The young man's cigar had gone out and he struck a match, puffing as he held the flame to the end which glowed red.

"No. Dad refuses to tell me."

"Then what can you do? The meeting is this weekend."

"There's always a way to climb a wall, Jonathan, no matter how tall that barrier might be. You just need to be devious enough."

"Devious? Are you planning something illegal?"

"Perhaps. Let's just say I take after my father in many ways."

Father and son smoked in silence.

Travis tensed as his mind wrestled with the details of the situation. *What could the old man have planned? If everyone is dead, nobody gets the keys. If nobody gets the keys, nobody gets the gold.*

The old man broke the silence. "So, if I can get G-pop to tell me the code word and the location of the gold, I'm very confident I'll be able to convince the solicitor to hand over the keys to me. "But your grandfather is toying with me. He knows I can only spend five minutes with him so he rambles on about family and friends and all that shit that is useless to him. You were his first and favorite grandchild. I think you can use that to your advantage and convince him to tell you the code word and location of the gold."

"He hasn't seen me since I was twenty-seven. He won't recognize me."

"He doesn't have to recognize you. The fact that the Life Beyond custodians are providing you entry into the facility is proof enough that you're his family."

"Ah, I see." The young man stroked his chin and nodded.

"Stick to the script I gave you, Jonathan, and everything will turn out just fine." The two men ground out their cigars and returned to the dining room.

Travis had listened to their conversation with great interest. Gold bullion would be an incredible prize if he was able to pull off the con. To succeed, he would need to impersonate the son. To pose as Jonathan, he would need to kidnap him, take his clothes, and other identifying papers. Based on the old man's words, the son planned to visit the facility the next day.

I need to act quickly.

Mr. Randall and Jonathan returned to their table, and the waiter freshened their brandies. Travis quietly left the restaurant while his server's attention was focused on another couple. He wandered the street until he located a parked cab outside a diner. The owner's cap lay on the seat. *Perfect,* Travis thought as he popped the lock, slid in, and hotwired the vehicle. He drove the cab near the restaurant and parked a block away. Then he waited patiently.

His easy marks exited the restaurant an hour later.

"Marcus, please hail us a taxi," The old man said to the doorman.

"Right away, Mr. Randall." The man tipped his hat and scanned the road for available cabs.

"As luck would have it, sirs, I'm free," Travis said as he approached the group. He nodded at the gentlemen and doffed his cap. He pointed at his taxi by the curb.

Marcus scowled as he eyed Travis. He'd never seen the man before.

But Travis quickly slid his palm into the doorman's hand. "I'm sure you won't mind if I help these two fine gentlemen since I'm already here." The doorman's eyes widened as he felt coins drop into his palm.

"Excellent service, Marcus," Mr. Randall exclaimed as he handed a twenty-dollar bill to the doorman. Pleasantly surprised at the double tip he'd just received, Marcus pocketed the cash and nodded politely at Mr. Randall.

"I'm parked right over here, sir," Travis explained as guided the gentlemen to the stolen taxi. He was eager to get on the road lest the owner finish dinner and discover his car was missing. He opened the door onto the sidewalk and nodded as the men climbed in."

"Where to?" he asked as he slid into the driver's seat.

"222 Spruce," Mr. Randall replied. "It's just a few blocks away. And, then you can take my son home at 363 Raven."

"Yes, sir. Right away, sir." Travis grinned as he started the engine and drove away.

The old man was deposited safely at his doorstep and watched the cab pull away. Ten blocks later, Travis pulled up to the son's townhome.

"Here we are, sir." Travis let the car idle as he scurried out and opened the door for the young man. As Jonathan stood to exit, Travis cold-cocked him over the head with the butt of his revolver and swiftly stuffed the unconscious man back into the cab. Travis glanced up and down the darkened street before climbing in and driving away.

The next day, he rubbed his swollen hands as he walked to the Life Beyond building. His knuckles were red and bleeding from beating Jonathan all night to get all the information he needed. As he neared the front door, he drew in a sharp breath. *Look confident,* he reminded himself.

"Good morning, sir. Can I help you," a security guard asked as Travis entered the lobby.

"Yes, I'm Jonathan Randall and I'm here to see my grandfather."

"I see," the officer said as he scanned his log. "Yes, I see you had a nine o'clock appointment." He glanced up. "Do you have the payment, sir?"

"My father prepaid for this visit. If you check your records, you'll find that he made the arrangement last week."

The man left and strode into the office where another security officer observed them. After consulting the records, the original officer returned. "Yes, sir. That's correct. We show payment in full. May I see your identification?"

Travis' stomach twisted in knots. He had the ID but hoped he transformed his appearance enough to match the photo. He slowly withdrew his wallet and extracted the card. He studied it before handing it to the officer. "Here you go. I must commend you on the thoroughness to ensure only the proper people gain access." He channeled Mr. Randall's mannerisms and confidence.

The officer smiled at him and took the card. "Yes sir, we try." He studied the ID and looked at Travis several times before he asked, "What's your birthday, sir?"

"June 16, 1927," he offered without hesitation.

"Thank you, sir. Let me show you the way." They walked through a series of three secure doors before entering a small room, the size of a walk-in closet. The officer motioned for Travis to sit. "I'll be back with George Randall. Please wait here."

Travis surveyed the cramp little room. Besides a counter and a stool, the space was void of any other decoration or furniture. He only had five minutes to get his answers. He had to be devious, craftier than an old dead man. He wasn't sure what he was going to encounter, but visions of Frankenstein leapt to mind.

The door knob rattled and the officer strode in carrying a small square case which he laid carefully on the counter. He rotated the metal box until the latch faced Travis. "Here's Mr. George Randall as you requested. Let me remind you that you only have five minutes. The time starts when you pop the latch and lift the lid. A timer on the box will close the lid. Is that clear?"

"Perfectly," Travis replied, his fingers twitching, eager to flip the latch.

"Fine, I'll leave you alone with your loved one."

Travis' breathing echoed in the tiny chamber, which was lit only by a bare bulb in the ceiling. Eerie shadows danced across the walls. The atmosphere thickened with the tension eking from Travis' pores. He sucked in a deep breath and then blew it out sharply. He whispered to himself, "Okay, Jonathan, you better have told me the truth."

Travis flipped the latch and lifted the lid. He jerked when he found a head staring at him. The head was perfectly preserved and showed every hair and imperfection. The eyes glared at him—bright green eyes. "Who are you?" it demanded.

Stay calm and stick to the script. "Hi G-Pop, it's Jonathan. Your grandson."

The head looked him up and down. "You are? I don't recognize you."

"I was twenty-seven when you died. I've changed a lot in the last twenty years." He quickly followed with, "Dad says hi!"

"Bastard," the head snarled. "Nothing but a bastard. He wants my gold."

"Wouldn't you want your family to benefit from your efforts?" Travis was pleased with his upbeat question. Prey on the old man's emotions.

"Fuck you all!" the head shouted. "The gold is mine."

"But G-Pop, we could put that money to good use."

"Like what? Name me one fucking thing you would do with my gold?"

"I'd give a lot to charity. Dad told me you died from cancer. I'd make sure some of your money goes toward finding a cure."

"Liar. My family spawned thieves and liars." The head squinted at Travis. "And, do you know who the biggest liar is?"

The clock was ticking and Travis needed to stay on point. "Who G-Pop?"

"You!" the old man barked. A sinister sneer creased his wrinkled face. "You don't know all the rules do you, young man?"

"Whatcha mean?" A shiver crept up Travis' spine.

"The strict rules for our little meeting?" The head chuckled. "Only family can visit. All others are forbidden under penalty of death."

"I know that. I am family. I'm your grandson." Travis remained calm, though his heart hammered furiously.

"You're pretending to be my grandson. Do you know what happens if you disobey the rules?"

Travis' palms sweated and he rubbed them on his pants. *The head is toying with me. He's just wasting time.* "Stop G-Pop, you're being silly," Travis' voice was calm and confident. He was going to see this ruse to the end no matter what.

"Am I? What color are my eyes?"

Travis peered at the head. "Bright green."

"What color are your father's eyes?"

Travis' mind raced. He'd learned so much about the son, he didn't bother to worry about the father. "Um, green, of course. Just like yours." His voice quavered but he hoped he still sounded confident.

The room went black and scuffling ensued.

Travis screamed.

Then all went quiet.

Eerily quiet.

The overhead light flickered back on and a figure stood staring at the head.

"What you didn't know," the figured hissed, "Was that I was never able to have children so we adopted our precious boy, Nathanial. His eyes are a gray blue just like yours should be. I do remember my grandson. And you are not him."

Travis felt peculiar. Initially, he had been staring at a head but now he was gazing up at a person that looked like him and talked like him. The sickening reality filled him with dread. Somehow his soul had been switched with Mr. Randall's.

Travis now resided inside the head.

"The penalty for outsiders is death," the figure explained. "You have provided the means for me to finally find my gold and live the life I deserve. You came to me as a penniless con man and you will stay locked in that head a penniless con man."

A soft tone sounded. "Ah, it looks as though our time is up. Such a pity. We were just getting to know one another." The figure turned to leave.

"Wait!" Travis croaked. "What happens to me?"

"I simply don't care. It feels great to be alive again. Goodbye." The figure turned and left the room.

The timer automatically closed and latched the box.

The guard returned, collected the case, and placed it back on the shelf with thousands of similar boxes.

George Randall stood outside Beyond Life and stared up into the cloudless sky. He flexed his arms and breathed the fresh spring air. "It's lovely to have a youthful body again. Muscles contracting and lungs expanding."

"I imagine it's a welcome relief from being cramped inside that head for the last twenty years. Welcome back, Dad," his son said as he forced a smile.

"That was quite a devious plan you hatched, Nathanial. It's a pity that you sacrificed my grandson just so that you could benefit."

"Don't preach to me. It was your idea to find a dimwitted stranger. Jonathan was merely collateral damage. Once I discovered that con man was listening to my conversation, I took full advantage of the opportunity. Travis Tinker was an easy mark for our plan."

"My plan," George Randall hissed.

"Yes, your plan. But my extraordinary execution. Once you have the keys, we'll collect the gold and we'll be the richest family in the United States."

"The world," George corrected. He drew in another deep breath, enjoying the sensation of the blood pumping throughout his body. Travis had provided him with a youthful physique, almost thirty years the junior to his own son who was approaching seventy.

George gazed at his son and mused about the future: *It won't be long before you die from old age. I have time on my side. I've been patient for twenty years, and I can wait a little longer.*

A Winner Every Time

For the third night in a row, Greg couldn't sleep. That cozy feeling of tumbling into unconsciousness evaded him once again.

Not that he didn't try.

Melatonin, sleeping potions, and eye masks had no effect on the constant barrage of thoughts racing through his mind. He tossed one way and then turned the other. He threw the covers off, then he pulled them up under his chin. He laid on his side, his back, and his stomach.

Nothing worked.

It was one in the morning. He'd been lying awake in bed for three hours. He flung the bedspread onto the floor and stared at the ceiling.

Nope, I'm not getting up, he told himself. But he wasn't convinced.

"A winner every time!" A computerized voice cheerfully called out to him.

"Leave me alone!" he screamed. Despite his response, he yearned to get up. Like a puppet on a string, he felt the pull to get out of bed and play a game, not on his own accord, but by the direction of some wicked entity that had crept into his mind. His fingers involuntarily twitched back and forth across the sheets as if they were moving buttons on a joystick. He knew it was a matter of time before he would give in to the program.

"Riches await you. Give it a try. You won't be disappointed." Clanging bells and electronic cheering drifted through the apartment.

"Go away! I wish I'd never started playing you!" Greg pressed the heels of his hands deep into his temples. *How did I get into this mess?*

Three days earlier, Greg had agreed to house sit while his co-worker, Jethro, flew to Cancun for a long weekend. The two men barely knew each other, so Greg had been surprised when Jethro approached him at work.

"I'm going on vacation for a few days and need someone to watch my fish. You don't mind, do you? I'll watch your house when you decide to take a vacation."

"Um," Greg had mumbled. Blindsided by the question, he fumbled for the right words to say no. Confrontations easily muddled his mind and silenced his voice.

"Great! I knew I could count on you." Jethro clapped him on the back and marched away.

Greg sat stunned. Seconds later, his mouth finally caught up. "I didn't really agree to watch your fish," he squeaked. But Jethro had already left the office.

The memory of that encounter streamed through Greg's head as he stood outside the door to Jethro's apartment. His co-worker had bulldozed him into watching his fish. But Greg hadn't said no either. He didn't know if he was more furious with himself or with Jethro.

Bitterness seethed behind his blank face when the door flew open and Jethro ushered him inside. "Hi, buddy. Come on in."

Greg hated being called buddy. Swallowing his unspoken words, he entered the room and looked around.

"Welcome to my casa. It's small but it has everything you need: a bed, food, drink, TV, and all the video games your little heart desires." Jethro pulled Greg to a black computer desk against the wall. Three large monitors filled the desk top while various peripherals, blinking and flashing, lined shelves above them.

An aficionado of fantasy books, Greg surveyed the equipment with disinterest. He'd rather sit quietly and read one of his paperbacks.

"Help yourself to the games," Jethro offered. "I have a package deal. I haven't used up all my credits, and you're welcome to use them. Payment for taking care of my fish."

"Great," Greg replied indifferently. He could care less about playing the stupid games.

"Oh, there is one little thing. Don't unlock the premium games. Just mess about with the ones I've already opened. Okay?"

Lost in thought wishing he was somewhere else, Greg didn't respond.

"Greg. Do you understand? Don't open the premium package. Seriously. That's taboo."

"Yep. I understand." *Get out of here and leave me alone.*

Jethro grabbed his tote and jacket and hurried to the door. "I almost forgot about the fish. Just a few shakes in the morning and afternoon. That's all the food they need. Otherwise, they just swim around and amuse themselves."

Greg nodded as he followed Jethro to the door. "Yep, I understand."

Once the door shut, Greg exhaled as though he'd been holding his breath the entire conversation. Finally, he was alone. He glanced around the cramped apartment. Black curtains draped crookedly across the small window. When he pulled them open, the curtain rod crashed to the floor kicking mini dust tornadoes in its wake.

Greg coughed and fanned the air. Broken metal brackets poked out of the wall where the rod had precariously perched. Studying the tangled heap on the floor, Greg surmised that Jethro had balanced the rod and had never intended to open the curtains. He shrugged and kicked the drapes to the wall.

Greg sat back in the recliner, grabbed the remote, and turned on the TV. Anticipating a premium movie subscription, his hope

turned to disappointment as he scrolled through the basic chan-
nels in the online guide.

This really sucks.

He clicked the remote off and tossed it onto the side table.

I'll check out the food and drink.

Except for miscellaneous bags of potato chips that he fished out
of a cabinet, the galley-style kitchen offered precious little except
for an assortment of cereal boxes lining one counter. Fifteen boxes
in total. Greg reviewed his options. Not one healthy alternative in
the collection of fruit-flavored nuggets and chocolate flakes that
boasted that they tasted like real chocolate.

Greg shook his head at the meager offerings. When he inspected
the refrigerator, his excitement on finding Belgium beer deflated
when several take-out containers toppled onto the floor. Ramen
noodles snaked amid slimy pink mold shimmering on question-
able meat and scary-looking vegetables. It took almost an entire roll
of paper towel to scoop the mess off the floor and dump it into a
garbage can under the kitchen sink.

Greg grabbed three beers and headed toward the computer desk.
The last thing he wanted to do was play a video game, but he hadn't
brought a book and there was nothing on television. With nothing
else to preoccupy his time, Greg turned the computer on and sat
back as the device powered up with a high-pitched whine. Soon,
the monitor flickered on.

A large rectangular icon twirled in the middle of the screen.
It appeared like a giant die angled on one end. Each side was a
different color and words flashed as the logo pirouetted.

"Care to play a game, Jethro?" a mechanical voice asked.

Greg squinted at the monitor. The creepy voice possessed inflections just like Jethro's Brooklyn accent. Not expecting an answer, Greg sarcastically responded, "No!" and reached for the mouse to see what else he could find on the PC.

Before he could make that move, he received a reply. "Hello, guest of Jethro. Perhaps you may be interested in something more exciting."

Icy fingers tickled his spine, and Greg pushed the chair away from the desk. He glared at the machine. *What strange hell is this?*

Always one to trust his instincts, Greg stood up and glanced toward the television. Reruns of an old TV show were better than dealing with an odd video game with a spooky voice. He turned toward the recliner.

"We have another winner! Don't you want to play?"

Startled, Greg stopped and peered at the computer. *It's as though the program knew what I was planning.*

"Unlock the premium games and get twenty free tries at the million dollars! A winner every hour!" The tone of the voice was changing. It was subtle, but Greg could swear the accent was changing to match his southern drawl.

What the hell?

The rectangular logo that had been twirling on the screen abruptly broke off into four square panels, each one spinning into a separate corner of the monitor. In order—red, blue, yellow, green—the panels flashed as words scrolled across their blocks.

I didn't touch anything. This is so weird.

"Greetings, Jethro's guest! Let's get started with a name. What's yours?"

Greg staggered backward. The program was unraveling his nerves. Just the voice, alone, was freaking him out. He glanced at the individual color blocks as they pulsed on the screen: CLASSIC GAMES, NUMBER GAMES, CARD GAMES, PREMIUM GAMES.

In the corner of each block was a lock symbol. Three of the panels were unlocked. The fourth panel, the one promoting premium games, displayed a locked symbol.

Suddenly, a crow with red eyes flew onto the screen. It carried a wad of bills in its beak. "Unlock the premium games and be a winner!" the synthesized voice goaded.

Jethro's words rang in Greg's mind, "Don't unlock the premium games."

I wonder why? What could be the harm?

Just as that thought danced in his head, the voice spoke again, "What's your name? All I need is your name so you can play games. What's the harm in that?"

Shit, that's what I was just thinking! How did the computer know that? Trembling, Greg glanced nervously around the room. Like the great and powerful Oz, he had hoped to find someone hiding somewhere and manipulating the computer at his expense.

Greg was alone.

Jethro must have some new artificial intelligence loaded on his gaming software, Greg thought. *But what version of AI can read minds?*

Before he realized what was happening, his hand slid around the mouse and toggled on CLASSIC GAMES. "What the hell!" he shouted as he tried to pry his hand away. But it stuck to the mouse as though it had been glued.

"Great choice!" the machine praised. "But first we need a name. Please speak your name now."

Despite his anxiety at the program's ability, Greg was intrigued by how it operated and decided to provide a fake name to test its functions. "GG," he responded.

Several moments passed before the red square for CLASSIC GAMES moved to the center of the screen and the name "Greg" scrolled through the red color block.

"Greg? I said GG, not Greg." He scowled at the blinking machine.

"Thank you for providing your name. You may commence playing the classic games." The voice's upbeat tone irritated Greg.

"Wait a minute! I said GG."

Silence.

He crept closer to the machine. The color blocks had stopped moving and no longer flashed. Several moments passed with no change. Thinking the program had permanently frozen, he turned to leave.

He had only taken a few steps when a familiar voice spoke. The accent and inflection were now an exact copy of his own. Greg's blood turned to ice.

"I knew you were lying, Greg. Now, let's play some games. You've entered the classic bundle. Please enjoy."

Dumbfounded, Greg stared at the monitor which had resumed its lilting music and flashing lights. "What the hell is happening?" he said under his breath.

His fingers twitched. The movement was insignificant like an involuntary tic. But then his left hand jerked outward as though tugged by unseen hands and then reached toward the joystick that was sitting on the desk. Alarmed, he tried to remove his hand but it wouldn't budge. Without warning, his other hand grabbed the swivel chair and rolled it in front of the PC.

"What's going on?" Greg demanded.

"Sit down, Greg. Time to play your games!" the cloying voice cajoled.

For a brief flick of time, he considered running out the door but couldn't move his feet. Something, or someone, had seized control and forced him to sit down. A prisoner in his own body, he could only stare mutely as his hands played the games. In the background, bells clanged and an electronic audience cheered him on.

Four hours later, he had played every one of the games in the classic and numbers bundles and was halfway through the card games. All the while, a melodic voice with a southern tinge kept encouraging him to play. "Great game, Greg! Let's play another."

His stomach growled. He hadn't eaten anything and the three beers he had originally toted to the desk, stood on the floor unopened. He leaned down to pick up a beer.

"You haven't finished your game, Greg." The diabolical voice scolded.

"Shut up!" Greg snapped. His body shook from exhaustion and resentment. "Just shut up. I'm tired, hungry, and thirsty."

Silence. Once again, the computer grew eerily quiet.

Greg grabbed a beer bottle and slammed its top on the edge of the desk. The metal cap flew off and rattled behind the monitor. He sipped the beer, smacked his lips, and then tipped the bottle back, gulping the contents all at once.

Sensing the program had released the hold on his body, he bolted from his seat, ran into the kitchen, and snatched a fruity nugget cereal. After carefully unfolding the flaps, he plunged both hands into the box and shoveled fistfuls of multi-colored morsels into his mouth.

He opened another beer and scarfed it down in no time at all, followed by a couple of handfuls of sweet cereal. Between the alcohol and sugar, Greg soon grew lethargic and sleepy. After finishing the third beer and a few fistfuls of cereal, he slumped back in the chair and stared listlessly at the screen.

"A winner every time!" the mechanical voice chirped. "Unlock the green square and win a million dollars."

With his senses dulled from the alcohol and sugar rush, Greg's head slowly fell forward until his forehead rested on the edge of the desk directly in front of the main monitor. Moments later, his raspy snore merged with the program's carnival-style music.

"Unlock the premium games and you'll be a winner in no time," the disembodied voice urged.

Greg's left hand jerked. The movement was hard enough to wake him, but he languished in a sleepy stupor. He grinned as his fingers spasmed and twitched up and down. His fuzzy mind couldn't comprehend why his hand was moving.

His right hand lurched to the side as though it had been violently tugged. Slowly it moved up to the mouse. Greg whimpered. Even in his dazed state, he knew his arms were being manipulated by the infernal program. And there was nothing he could do to stop it.

"Just click the green square, Greg," the voice demanded.

Greg squeezed his eyes and summoned all his strength to stop his hand. But it grabbed the mouse anyway, hovered the cursor over the premium games, and clicked the green block.

That was three days ago.

Now, as Greg lay in bed and stared at the ceiling, an irresistible urge to play the game gnawed at his sleep-deprived brain. His fingers twisted and pulled at the sheets.

"Time to play, Greg. A winner every time."

After three days of no sleep, Greg no longer cared about anything. He wore the same clothes as the first day he arrived. Two fish, having succumbed to lack of food, floated at the top of the tank, and empty beer bottles and discarded cereal boxes littered the floor.

"A winner every..."

"Shut up! I'm coming you piece of shit!" Greg rolled out of bed and fell to the floor with a *thud*. Exhaustion sapped his strength.

Not able to stand, he crawled on his hands and knees until he reached the computer desk. He swept his arm in a wide arc along the floor and whacked empty bottles and boxes out of the way. Using the desk as support, he finally stood up, wavered in front of the monitor, and then collapsed into the chair.

His right hand automatically grabbed the mouse and began scrolling through the premium games.

"You've exhausted Jethro's credits. You must now add more money to continue your play." The mechanical voice wasn't as cheerful as it was in previous days.

"I don't have any money," Greg hissed before adding, "You can't get blood out of a stone."

"Perhaps there's a way."

The words curled through Greg's mind like a wriggling, spine-covered worm. A sudden need to vomit boiled up from his belly, and he grabbed the trash can from under the desk just as an explosion of mush burst out of his mouth. He swiped the chunks from his face with the back of his hand.

"Leave me alone. I'm done. I don't want to play anymore." Greg crumpled to the floor and began crawling away.

Sparks shot out of the monitor like miniature fireworks, followed by a long, unnatural squeal. Its high-pitched whine curdled Greg's blood. He glanced over his shoulder just as a phantom arm emerged from the screen. The wispy appendage coiled like a snake and stretched toward Greg.

"Get away from me!" he cried as the specter floated toward him. Transparent bony fingers unfurled and reached for Greg as he squirmed along the floor like a frightened lizard.

"Don't leave just yet, Greg," the program warned as ghostly fingers wrapped around one leg and pulled him back to the desk. "Now, let's talk about that payment."

Greg lay panting on the floor. "But I don't have money and I'm tired." He closed his eyes and wheezed.

"Ah, but you have something much more valuable."

A piercing shriek exploded from the computer. Greg's eyes flew open. "No!" he screamed as he stared into a skeletal face hovering inches from his nose. Large, yellow eyes filled the eye sockets and a black, forked tongue slithered between its missing front teeth and licked Greg's cheek.

"Your soul is adequate payment," the specter hissed. Cadaver fingers dug into Greg's fleshy arms and lifted him toward the phantom's gaping maw.

"Nooooo!"

"Hello, I'm home!" Jethro yelled as he pushed into the apartment. When he entered, a pungent odor punched him in the face. He held his nose and grimaced. Piles of bottles and cereal boxes littered the floor. Everything was in disarray. A few dead fish floated on the surface of the tank, the curtains had been pulled down, and garbage was strewn everywhere. *What the hell happened here?*

"Hello, Greg?" he hollered.

Silence.

"Hi buddy, I'm home. Where are you?" Jethro dropped his tote in the bedroom and checked for his missing friend. Finding nobody, he walked back into the living room. "Are you still here?"

"Shit," Jethro cursed. "Looks like you went home and left me with this mess. Thanks a lot, buddy!"

He grabbed a heavy-duty trash bag and worked his way over to the computer desk. The stench got worse. "Damn. What is that smell?" He kicked debris out of the way. The movement awakened the computer and it displayed the bright green block of the premium bundle with an unlocked symbol. "Greg, what the hell did you do? I told you not to mess around with the premium games."

As Jethro drew closer to the monitor, he gagged and reeled backward. Something was obviously rotting. Movement caught his attention. As he studied a pile of trash in front of the desk, debris tumbled to the floor.

"What the hell!" he yelled.

After several seconds, Jethro reached forward. His finger trembled as it stretched toward the pile that had shifted earlier. Cautiously, he flicked bits of trash to the floor. Then he tugged on a wedged cereal box. Like a key piece in a wooden puzzle tower, removing the box caused a landslide of debris.

Jethro screamed.

Greg, or what remained of him, sprawled in front of the monitor. Dead eyes had sunken back into their sockets. Long strands of bloody drool stretched between his mouth, eyes, and the screen. His skin clung to his frame like parchment paper as though every drop of moisture had been removed from his body. A black tongue pushed out of his mouth, slid over his scabby lips, and then retreated back into the toothy hole.

While his skeletal right hand gripped the mouse, the bony fingers of his left tapped the buttons on the joystick.

A cheerful voice called out from the computer. "We have a winner! Congratulations, Greg! Do you want to play double or nothing?"

The slack-jaw corpse slowly nodded his head up and down. "Yes!" it screeched.

A Murder of Crows

"**D**amned crows!" Bruce growled as he staggered through the cornfield. He slid his air rifle into position and aimed.

Pop, pop, pop.

"Get off my fuckin' land!" The black birds scattered into the surrounding oak trees and chuckled at him. He scowled back.

He pulled a whiskey nips out of his pocket, twisted the cap, and sucked the contents in one quick gulp. His overalls could easily hold eight of the tiny plastic nips, which came in handy when he had chores all day. This was the last one. Holding the bottle up in the fading light, he eyed it for any remaining drops. For good measure, he ran his pinkie around the rim and then slid it across his tongue.

Time to head home. He tossed the bottle into the cornstalks and trudged back to the farmhouse as the crows taunted him from their safe perches.

Jen better have dinner ready. I'm starving, he thought as he stumbled for home.

Lost in a happy daydream, Jen watched the flock of crows glide over the cornfield as she twirled the silver band on her ring finger. The black birds flew effortlessly through the sky, and she envied their freedom, their happy-go-lucky life. Then she spied Bruce lurching past the chicken coop. A sneer darkened his face. He wasn't happy. He was never happy.

She lightly touched her right eye, a bruised reminder of what happens if she doesn't do what Bruce demands, if she doesn't make Bruce happy. She whirled and limped to the stove. Water for the potatoes boiled over and hissed as it ran onto the burner. "Oh no," she wailed. She grabbed a towel and quickly cleaned the mess just as Bruce barged through the kitchen door.

"Honey, I'm home!" he bellowed. Jen knew he was drunk. He bumped into her as he staggered to the sink. "What's for dinner tonight? Same old shit or have you learned to finally cook?" He threw his head back and cackled. "Cook...that's a laugh. I should have made sure you knew how to cook before I made that deal with your daddy."

Jen was only sixteen when her father, Stan, had married her off to forty-year-old Bruce for a sum of one hundred dollars and two chickens. Her daddy was a drunk and a cheat, and he boasted he had a young'un in almost every house and almost as many stills hidden in the mountains.

The marriage deal had been struck on the front porch while he and Bruce drained a jug of home brew. Bruce had lamented that he really missed having a woman around the house. "I ain't had good cookin' for a while and the house is a pigsty."

Bruce's wife had mysteriously died. Gossipers whispered that she had knotted a bedsheet around her neck and leaped from the top beam in the barn. Her neck had snapped instantly. When Bruce had found her, she had a huge grin on her face. She was finally free from his beatings.

"How can I make you feel better?" Stan consoled. At that same moment, Jen walked onto the porch and hefted another jug of 'shine onto the table. Bruce smiled at her but she averted her eyes. "Now, be kind to your neighbor, Jen. Give him a smile, and let him see those brilliant blue eyes," her father ordered. Jen peered shyly at Bruce. He pursed his lips together in a mock kiss. She immediately felt dirty and turned to leave, but her father grabbed her arm.

"Now, don't run away, Jen, not just yet."

That's how her union with Bruce had started two years ago. Now eighteen, Jen had suffered two miscarriages (the result of severe beatings), had had her nose broken twice, and had fractured her left ankle when Bruce had chained her to the chicken coop all night for not having dinner ready on time.

The rusted metal chain had been tight, but Jen had reasoned she could wriggle her foot through the manacle with the help of slick chicken poop. The smelly lubricant wasn't enough, so she braced her hands on the ground and yanked to free her foot. The pain had been excruciating, but she had to get away. She'd rather suffer a broken ankle than stay with Bruce.

CRACK!

The ankle twisted to one side. With adrenalin masking her pain, she shoved her bent foot through the shackle. An oak branch proved to be an excellent staff to lean on as she hobbled into the night toward freedom.

Bruno, their old mutt hound, awoke to the commotion and yapped and yodeled in all directions, awakening Bruce. When he dashed outside, he noticed Jen was missing from the chicken coop. His anger rose quickly, beginning with his hands that scrunched into meaty fists to his jaws that bunched and clenched, popping a lopsided sneer across his face.

The full moon illuminated the cornstalks like a spotlight, and Bruce spied movement several yards into the field. It didn't take long for Bruce to catch up with Jen. Snatching her long black hair, he dragged her back to the house as she screamed and cried, "Bruce let me go. Please let me go!"

Behind closed doors, Jen's cries continued into the night until she finally lost consciousness.

In the four months since that assault, her ankle had healed enough that she could finally place weight on it. It ached constantly, and she had a noticeable limp, but she was alive.

Bruce staggered to the table, plopped down in his chair, and leaned against the slatted back. The rickety wood creaked from the strain. He watched Jen mash the potatoes in a large ceramic bowl. Warm, savory aromas filled the kitchen as pork chops and green beans warmed in the oven.

Bruce suddenly tilted forward and the chair legs stomped the floor with a loud thud. He grabbed the fork from the table and dug under his nails with one tine. "What time is it?" he asked without looking up.

Jen looked nervously at the clock on the wall. "About five-fifteen," she answered as she continued mashing.

"Five fucking fifteen!" he howled. "How many times do I need to remind you that dinner is on the table at FIVE O'CLOCK!" Bruce stood up and threw the fork at Jen. It narrowly missed her throat and clattered onto the counter. Frozen in fear, Jen stared at Bruce who sprang upon her. "When the fuck will you ever learn!"

Her grabbed her hair and yanked her down to the ground. The ceramic bowl and potatoes crashed to the floor. Bruce dragged Jen to the door as she kicked and screamed, her hands clawing at his fists. He threw the door open and pulled her squirming body over the threshold, which ripped her shirt and the skin from her back.

"When will you learn!" Bruce hollered as he stormed toward the chicken coop.

"Please, Bruce. Please!" Jen pleaded.

The liquor fueled his anger like gasoline on a bonfire. He dragged her by the woodpile, which snagged her clothes and yanked her from his grasp. "Fuckin' bitch!" he bellowed. Scooping her up, he tossed her over his shoulder and marched away as Jen kicked and scratched. Her fighting only made him more furious, and when they reached the chicken coop, he violently threw her to the ground.

SNAP.

Jen cried out and clenched her side where pain exploded throughout her torso, making it hard for her to breathe. She feared passing out.

Unchecked rage ignited. Unmoved by her pleas to stop, Bruce muttered to himself as he uncoiled the massive chain and viciously attached it to her injured ankle, wrenching her foot one way and then the other.

"Bruce, please," Jen gasped.

Chickens squawked and fluttered off their perches as Bruce's violent energy rolled over them in a monstrous negative wave. Some frightened hens managed to escape the wire enclosure and raced into the cornfield clucking urgently for help.

In the distance, soft caws responded to their calls.

Bruce cinched the chain around her ankle and hissed, "You can rot out here as far as I'm concerned. Now, I'm going to eat my fuckin' dinner." He trudged back to the house and slammed the kitchen door.

Trembling, Jen lay still and gasped from the agony that gripped her ribcage. Chickens flocked around her head. They clucked and lightly pecked at her hair. Some fluttered their soft wings against her cheeks. A gentle smile drifted across Jen's face as she drifted in and out of consciousness. Each time her eyes opened, she saw more hens standing guard around her.

All will be okay.

The chorus of voices drifted through her brain like a soft caress. She opened her eyes to find more chickens had huddled along her body, fanning her with their feathers and cooing murmurs of encouragement.

CAW!

Jen's eyes shot open at the booming squawk. A large black crow had landed on the ground nearby. It flapped its wings, and the hens parted as the corvid stepped closer and peered into Jen's bright, blue eyes.

On the verge of unconsciousness, her mind tilted. *Are you real?*

Her fingers twitched as she willed them to reach for the bird only inches from her face. The effort took all her mental and physical strength but, when she finally touched it, she was happily surprised by the velvety softness of its ebony feathers. *You're real!* The crow didn't resist as she tenderly stroked it.

"Help me," Jen croaked. "Help me escape." Exhausted from the effort, her hand fell to the ground.

The crow spread its wings wide and squawked.

CAW-CAW! CAW-CAW!

Soon, the surrounding trees filled with hundreds of crows cawing to their brother on the ground. The cacophony lasted several minutes before transitioning into a low warbling chant that consisted of human words layered with avian syllables. The chorus rose in pitch as the crows sang an encouragement to Jen: *Escape, take flight, escape.*

She batted her weak, tired eyes toward the murder of crows. *Are you really talking? Talking to me?*

CAW!

The large bird beside her waggled his tail and clacked his bill to grab her attention. Then it extended one wing, plucked a feather, and gently laid it onto her outstretched hand.

She instinctively curled her fingers around it and whispered, "Thank you."

CAW!

Jen knew she was dying and welcomed it as a relief from the pain and misery she had suffered at the hands of her cruel husband. Holding the crow feather in her hand had, somehow, become the catalyst to releasing her grip on the physical world. She sighed at the anticipation of crossing the veil.

Jen had always imagined that when she died, she would take flight into the sky—whether that be an angel or feathered creature—and she would finally know the freedom she had always yearned for.

She closed her eyes for the final time.

Sensations rippled through her like the gentle waves of an ocean sliding back and forth along a sandy beach. First, she became heavy, and then she felt light. Then an intense tingling spread throughout her body as though an army of ants marched along her skin.

Gradually, she drifted upward several feet before sinking back to the earth.

If this is what death brings, I welcome it.

The throbbing pain abruptly vanished, replaced by a welcoming warmth that penetrated deep into her soul. Torrents of suppressed emotions burst forth and surrounded her in a bright white light that illuminated her body as it lifted upward. Her back arched and her arms dropped to either side. Momentarily detained by the chain around her ankle, she hovered in the air for several seconds before it eventually slipped off, and she continued to rise upward.

I am now free and can fly with the others.

In the distance the black birds continued their chant: *Escape, take flight, escape.*

Bruce awoke with a pounding headache. "Where's my whiskey?" he muttered as he trashed the kitchen looking for his precious bottles. "I bet that bitch hid them. JEN!"

He stopped.

He had forgotten about last night. The spilled potatoes, the late dinner, the chicken coop.

He flung the kitchen door open and stumbled outside. Hundreds of crows taunted him from the oak trees. "I'll deal with you filthy birds later," he snarled as he neared the wire enclosure.

The chickens sensed his anger and scrambled to safe perches and cackled at him.

Did they just laugh at me? He eyed the hens suspiciously and then searched for Jen.

Bruce froze.

The thick chain lay abandoned on the ground, and Jen was nowhere to be seen. Traces of blood dotted the dirt, and black, fledgling feathers fluttered everywhere. *There's no way she could get out of this...not this time,* he thought as he examined the rusted chain.

CAW!

Bruce whirled toward the sound and found himself eye-to-eye with a sleek, black crow perched on the coop's corrugated roof. Cold fingers of fear stroked the length of his spine. There was something unusual about this bird. He staggered backward as his mind raced. *I must still be drunk,* he reasoned.

He licked his lips and leaned closer. The bird cocked its head and stared back at him. It wasn't his imagination, this crow had brilliant blue eyes, the same color as Jen's, and a narrow silver band encircled one of its legs.

CAW!

The crow launched straight at Bruce's face. Its talons raked his forehead, while its large beak stabbed into both of his eyes. Then it soared high into the sky and joined its brothers and sisters swirling in a large, black mass.

"You fuckin' bitch! I'll get you!" Bruce cried out. Blinded by the attack he waved his hands back and forth in front of his body as he felt for anything that would guide him back toward the house.

The blue-eyed crow attacked again and jabbed into his right ear, plunging deep into his ear drum.

"Shit!" He lashed out at the bird but it easily flew out of harm's way and rejoined the flock. Blood streamed down Bruce's face and neck as he looked skyward with sightless eyes. He raised his fist in defiance and screamed, "You fuckin' birds!"

The murder of crows dropped from the sky like a feathered missile approaching its target. They engulfed the flailing man and pecked and clawed until he fell dead to the ground. Then the flock darted skyward except for one bird: the crow with the bright blue eyes and silver band around one leg.

She stood upon his chest and gazed at her silent tormentor. In one final act of revenge, she detached the silver ring from her leg and dropped it into his gaping mouth. Then she soared into the heavens toward freedom.

Thank You

Thank you for taking the time to read **Tales From the Crows**.

Please take a moment to write a review.

It's so important for a book to have social proof, and I'd love your help sharing this series with others who embrace their magic.

Leave a review or star rating at your favorite book retailer

For new releases, giveaways, and fun info, subscribe to my newsletter by visiting www.cllavigne.com

Acknowledgements

My readers rock. Your curiosity about all things magical sustains me.

My husband, Chris, is the most amazing person. Besides assuaging my doubts, he also makes time to review and comment on my stories.

And to my spirit animal, Josephine, you and your family contributed greatly to the tales that appear on these pages.

About Author

Born in Alaska and raised in England, CL is an Elemental Specialist who writes magical realism novels that have witch fantasy overtones. Her stories feature real people and natural magic, all controlled by the Spirits of Nature and otherworldly beings.

Residing in the Sunshine State with her husband, four cats and four goldfish, CL incorporates elements of magic, mysticism and mythology into her writings. It's not unusual to encounter dragons, elemental spirits, Leotes (glowing orbs) and even Big Foot as you follow her characters on their adventures.

Her current fantasy series is Chronicle of Ceres, which will feature 6 books. Books 1 – 3 are available at your favorite book retailer.

Embrace your magic!

Find the magic and stay informed about special deals, give-aways, new releases and other great updates by subscribing to her **NEWSLETTER**.

Discover CL's magic:

www.cllavigne.com

www.facebook.com/CLLaVigneAuthor

www.instagram.com/cllavigneauthor/

Also By

Chronicle of Ceres Magical Realism Series

Beginning of Tomorrows, book 1

Denali Rising, book 2

Shasta Beckons, book 3

Bluestone Shadows, book 4 (will release in 2024)

Tales From the Crows

Horror short story collection